PANDEMIC

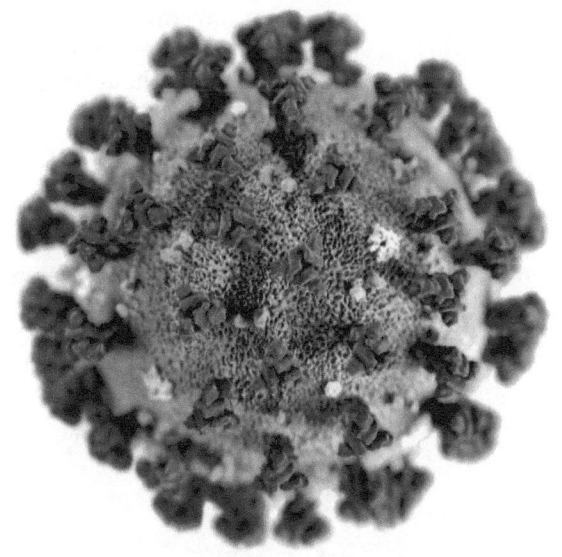

Scott Tilley, Ph.D.

PANDEMIC

Published by the Anthology Alliance

**Anthology
Alliance**

An imprint of Precious Publishing, LLC

Precious Publishing
www.PreciousPublishing.biz

ISBN-13: 978-1-951750-06-0
ISBN-13: 978-1-951750-07-7 (ebook)

TABLE OF CONTENTS

DEDICATION

To all the first responders, health care professionals, and frontline workers deemed essential during the pandemic.

(xyfen / Shutterstock.com)

PREFACE

The beginning of 2020 saw the emergence of the SARS-CoV-2 novel coronavirus and the rise of COVID-19. This worldwide pandemic has changed our lives dramatically. We have to look back over 100 years, to 1918 and the Spanish Flu pandemic, for a comparable period in the world's history. We've been forced into quarantine, witnessed the spread of the disease around the globe, and experienced an economic downturn the likes of which we haven't seen since the Great Depression in the 1930s.

We're still trying to adjust to the new normal – whatever that means. Even our vocabulary has changed. We're pinning our hopes on the development of a vaccine, but what if this is more like the medieval Black Death, the great pestilence that kept coming back?

This book provides a glimpse into how people have dealt with the COVID-19 pandemic. Many lives were lost, many businesses went bust, but one thing became crystal clear: the value of family and friends is eternal.

Scott Tilley
Melbourne, FL
November 28, 2020

ACKNOWLEDGEMENTS

The COVID-19 pandemic has taught us some valuable lessons. For example, people working hard in the service industry are essential to keeping society going. They are paid poorly for their work, but without their efforts, store shelves would be empty and everything we take for granted in our modern economy would grind to a halt. From those of us who have the luxury of working from home: Thank You.

If there is one group of professionals that should be acknowledged for performing above and beyond the call of duty, it is folks toiling away in health care. To doctors, nurses, orderlies, long term care attendants, and everyone else who has been stretched to the limit over the past few months of the pandemic: Thank You.

This is a somewhat unique anthology in that I am both a contributing author and the managing editor. I want to thank everyone who submitted their work for consideration of inclusion in the book; without them, this wonderful collection would not exist. Any errors that remain in the text are solely my responsibility.

A BETTER DAY

Anne Bonner

Sitting alone in twilight's stillness

Under the tall magnolia tree

Laden with creamy blossoms

I inhale the gentle spiciness of the air

Thoroughly enjoying the great outdoors

I envy the birds' freedom

As they fly back to their nests for the night

Darkness descends and the moon's golden beams

A shroud wraps around me

Comforting me

With alarming alacrity

The COVID-19 pandemic panic spread

Its flu-like virus the world over

Killing thousands of innocent people

How could countries be prepared

For an unknown disease, lab created?

Mixed messages from learned ones

Wear a mask   don't wear a mask

Wash hands twenty seconds with anti-bacterial soap

Perhaps wear gloves

Social distancing six feet apart

Only essential establishments in the U.S. were open

Liquor stores considered essential

Churches non-essential

Public schools are out

Many private schools forevermore shuttered

Graduation Day an unhappy forever memory

What's in store for the Fall?

Some U.S. Governors are content

For their states' populations to remain shut-in

Causing unrest in already volatile situations

Let the people out

Time to open the economy

Being shut-in for months

I dream of cruising the open sea

Visiting Europe   ancient artifacts   beautiful cathedrals

I dream of seeing the Wailing Wall of Jerusalem

The temples and mosques of Iran

It's the interaction with the peoples that is enjoyable

Their customs and their cuisines

Having lived in the Philippines

I would like to revisit Manila

And the mountain village of Bagio

My mouth waters for some of my favorite foods

Lumpia   chicken adobo   fried rice

So much to see and do

Dream on!

Midnight clouds the luminous sky

Muddying my thoughts

The soughing wind moans

I grieve   I live   I fill my lungs with fresh air

Before ambling back to my feather bed in my home

My prison

I have scribbled all I have to say

An ode to those the world over

Who have the coronavirus

I pray for those thousands of poor souls

Who have succumbed

Passing through earth's orbit to Heaven above

I pray tomorrow will be a better day

The dawn of a new era!

About the Author

Anne Bonner is a fifth-generation Floridian who has lived all over the world with her fighter-pilot husband.

She has published ten historical fiction books in ten years, all set in the early wilds of Florida. Anne attended schools in Cocoa and the University of Florida. She's a former Board member of the Brevard Heritage Council and the Space Coast Writers' Guild. Anne is also a member of the American Pen Women and the Florida Historical Society.

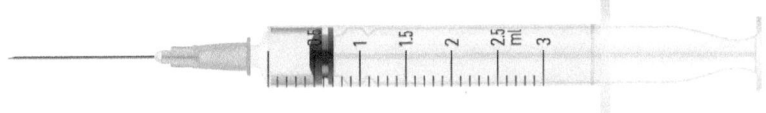

People wait in line for a COVID-19 test at a COVID-19 Assessment Centre in Scarborough, Ontario, Canada on September 29, 2020. (Bob Hilscher / Shutterstock.com)

Testing was a constant challenge for most countries, and the messaging regarding testing asymptomatic people was inconsistent. The nasal swab (PCR) tests are still the gold standard, but very unpleasant to experience.

PANDEMIC

"We have it totally under control. It's one person coming in from China. We have it under control. It's going to be just fine."

President Trump. January 22, 2020

NO LAUGHING MATTER

Ruth Coe Chambers

I've always believed in the healing power of laughter, and I've tried very hard to find something to laugh about during this pandemic. Where is that special spark to make people laugh, to make the elderly (yes, that's me) love the four walls we stare at each day? The four walls that may shield us from the dreaded COVID-19. It's no longer noteworthy on "The Today Show" that a person may be old but can still get around while being hunted by the coronavirus. Who will the virus strike next? There's nothing funny about people dying.

Today, age is noteworthy only when its wrinkled inhabitants have avoided the coronavirus. They've sheltered in place, not to avoid a bomb but a virus. Maybe you're one of those couples who have spent their life savings on a luxurious bomb shelter. All those cans of vegetables and containers of noodle soup stand erect as soldiers on their shelves waiting for a bomb that never came and a virus that can't even be seen. Just one more room to clean.

It seems, too, that trapped in this pandemic that caught us unawares, the people who need it most have no sense of humor. How about those lovely scarves Dr. Brix wears? Has anyone yet asked where she finds an endless supply of them, or how Nancy Pelosi creates a mask to match every outfit? Perhaps a little Singer tucked under her bed? And where do some find the happy transformations available in a beauty shop that can't or won't open its doors? But the important question is for Dr. Lysol. Does it taste better than it looks? Does it work inside out?

We muddle along without serious hope or a light at the end of the tunnel, but I have found the pot of gold at the end of the rainbow. Yes, you might be surprised that such is the joy, humor, and hope in my lucky find.

I'm going to marry Dr. Fauci when all this is over. He doesn't know it yet, nor does my husband, but if I can shelter in place for months on end, surely I can find a way to woo Dr. Fauci. Before he lost favor – it's easier to lose than laughter at the political level – I nearly got a crick in my neck trying to see Dr. Fauci's left hand on the television screen. My dreams came true when I finally saw that his left hand was not graced with a wedding ring. It would have been no laughing matter if it had because a dear friend had already fashioned a topper for the wedding cake. Two dolls of marzipan to represent Dr. Fauci and me. She made my wedding dress from duct tape, but her heart was in the right place. If it didn't work out, I could always eat the marzipan.

***

"What?"

So he is shorter than I am! At my age, I'm shrinking fast anyway. He's smart, but then I'm no trophy wife.

It may never come to pass, but even if I can't laugh, I can dream, can't I? And while I dream, I hope someday we all wake up to four walls that echo laughter and the hope that Dr. Fauci tries to bring us every day.

About the Author

Ruth Coe Chambers takes pride in her Florida panhandle roots that have inspired much of her writing.

Her work has appeared in print and online magazines as well as in anthologies. She has authored two prize-winning plays and has written three novels. Her third novel, *House on the Forgotten Coast*, won the Royal Palm Literary Award in 2018. She is currently writing *The Receding Tide* to complete her Bay Harbor Trilogy.

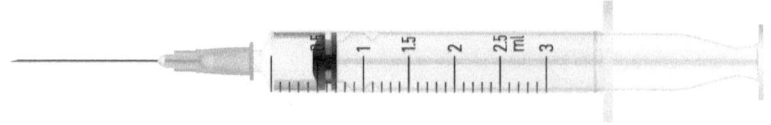

PANDEMIC

The pandemic dramatically increased the use of telemedicine. Patients were able to avoid in-person visits to hospitals and clinics and speak with their doctor online. It worked very well, considering how fast the technology was rolled out. (fizkes / Shutterstock.com)

PANDEMIC

Canadian Health Minister Patty Hajdu said even if Canada blocked all travel to and from China, people could find alternative routes and lie about where they've been, making it even harder to screen people coming in.

"The long-term implications of shutting down borders is one, they're not very effective in controlling disease, as in fact they're not effective at all," she said.

Patty Hajdu. February 6, 2020

As of November 27, 2020, the Canadian border with the United States remains closed.

I Had To

Nancy Clark

I needed to write this down to get it out in the open.

I am sad because I cannot reach out to hug all those I love, my children, my grandchildren, my mother, and my closest friends.

I feel blue as I cannot sit down with my aging mother and hold her hand or talk to her face-to-face.

Sad as I am unable to dine with my closest friends, have conversations, or watch movies.

I am blue because I can longer go to the places I want to visit as they are closed.

I wish people would heed what is being said by those brilliant minds who tell us the steps we need to take to keep this virus in check and to stop its spread.

So that once again, I can reach out to those I love and hug them tight, sit down next to my mother, go to visit with friends to enjoy a meal and conversation, and visit those places I long to see.

And most of all maybe, just maybe, we will survive this if we would only listen!

About the Author

Nancy Clark has been writing since she was in second grade. Her first poem was published in her school's literary book called *The Treasure Chest* when she was only eight years old. She has published four books: *Haiku for You, Haikus and Cinquains, Mini Sagas – Fifty Words or Bust,* and *Rainy Day Reads.* As a member of the Brevard Scribblers, she has had several of her short stories and poems published in their yearly anthology called *Driftwood.*

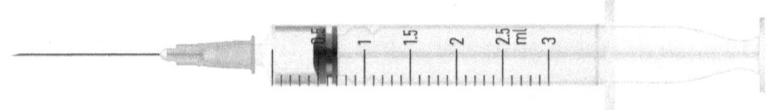

PANDEMIC

A crowded railway station in Wuhan, China on July 5, 2019 – before the pandemic. The coronavirus is widely believed to have originated in a live seafood market in Wuhan. (Maciej Zarzeczny / Shutterstock.com)

PANDEMIC

"We have therefore made the assessment that COVID-19 can be characterized as a pandemic.

Pandemic is not a word to use lightly or carelessly. It is a word that, if misused, can cause unreasonable fear, or unjustified acceptance that the fight is over, leading to unnecessary suffering and death."

WHO Director Dr. Tedros Ghebreyesus. March 11, 2020.

BORDERS

Anne-Marie Derouault

We're living historical times

Borders closed

No more flights to connect my two countries

For at least thirty days

Unheard of

In twenty years of Florida living

Extraordinary times.

Tears came

While reading the announcement yesterday

Late evening... again... too late

Of course

We will survive. For now,

Take care of myself

Curl up on the beach

Listen to sacred chants

Carry the image of a Mediterranean cove

Deep within

Call on it often.

Calm and collected

Stay home

Fortunately there is a garden

Which saved me before

And will save me again

Big trees

One can hold out for a long time

In the company of the trees

Water for swimming

Relaxing the body

That day when the world woke up

Split into several continents, suddenly

Separate and disconnected

How to take it?

Well, take it well

Take it gracefully

For there is no other choice.

About the Author

Anne-Marie Derouault was born in Paris and now lives in Florida. She is a consultant in management, communication, and stress reduction. She writes free verse poetry in French and in English, haikus, and short stories, which are inspired by her love of travel, nature, and human beings. She recently published her first book, *While the Poem Lasts,* a bilingual collection of inspirational poetry. She is a member of Cape Canaveral Pen Women, Space Coast Writers' Guild, and Brevard Scribblers.

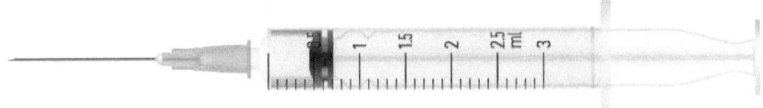

PANDEMIC

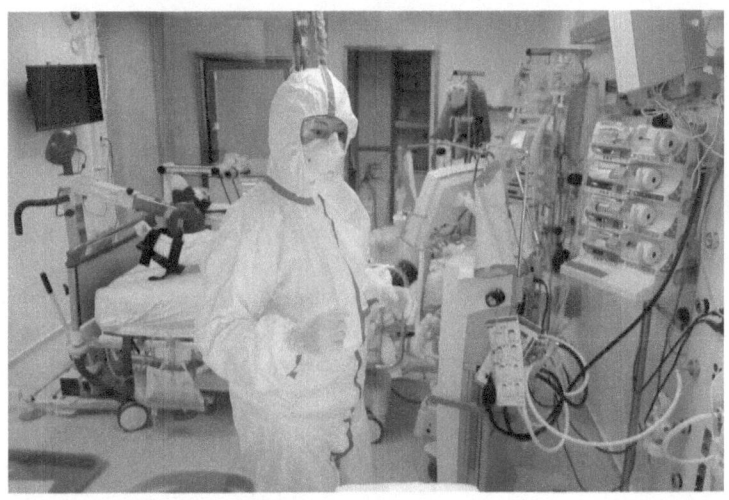

Medical staff work in the Intensive Care Unit (ICU) for COVID-19 patients in University Hospital of Liege in Belgium on May 5th, 2020. (Alexandros Michailidis / Shutterstock.com)

Overrunning the healthcare system was a constant worry for all countries during the pandemic. Some countries, such as the UK, seemed to prioritize their national healthcare system (NHS) over the economy at the start of the pandemic with their slogan "'Stay Home, Protect the NHS, Save Lives."

PANDEMIC

"I think, looking at it all, that we can turn the tide within the next 12 weeks and I'm absolutely confident that we can send coronavirus packing in this country."

Prime Minister Boris Johnson. March 19, 2020.

This was four days before the first national lockdown in the UK. As of the time of writing (November 27, 2020), the UK is in their second lockdown and will soon enter a tiered system.

2020 Isolation Olympics

Betty Whitaker Jackson

During March and April, Covenant Church in Palm Bay, Florida sponsored a competition for families to pass the time during the "stay at home" period. The Olympic Games had just been postponed. Kids could not return to school after spring break. Store shelves were emptying. Nonessential workers were home, elderly family members were vulnerable and isolated, and life changed with each news report.

Our church families were challenged with sixty activities, reported their accomplishments with videos and photos at a Facebook group site, raced to meet deadlines, and competed for prizes. (Rolls of toilet paper!)

As one of the finalists, I wrote a poem as a tiebreaker. It mentions some of the problems I solved, such as a Rube Goldberg invention, a science project, serving breakfast in bed, a card-built tower, a LEGO alligator, stacking household items to the ceiling, memorizing and reciting a Scripture passage and favorite verses, stretching raised arms in a husband/wife human pyramid, and creating shadow puppets.

The project provided much-needed family activities, introduced us to church members we may not have known, allowed for creativity and showing talents, and helped ease the tensions caused by the sudden lockdown when children couldn't return to school, and parents, many of whom were furloughed too, scrambled for meaningful activities for everyone to do.

Several words had to be used for the tiebreaker as part of the final video; they are in capital letters.

2020 Isolation Olympics to the Rescue

We couldn't have known the awaiting catastrophe,
China's CATAWAMPUS rumpus we'd see,
March's lion-like madness attacked us, it seemed,
Corona virus, SARS, COVID-19.

China's Wuhan flu became quite the thing,
stole our breath, exhaled fear, suffocated spring.
Science experts converged, worldwide, they asked,
"How do we treat it?" "Defeat it?" "Such a major task!"

Sore throat, tight breathing, fever, and chills,
inflammation, filled lungs; this quickly kills.
Watch out for high temps, a vicious strangling cough,
HAND SANITIZER, brisk washing might ward this off.

School's out, Hooray! Spring's LONG holiday

"Gatherings canceled." "Quarantine," experts say.
"Shelter in place." "Wipe down surfaces."
"Safe practices, observe,"
"wear masks," "avoid neighbors," "flatten the curve."

Hospitals, ICUs, tents, ships provide beds,
to mount an attack, it fills us with dread.
This contagious enemy, its ravages we see.
Store shelves are empty, "We're outta TP!"

Talking heads spread panic; case numbers are rising.
Birks, Fauci, the President all say it's surprising.
The number of outbreaks, how quickly it spreads.
Nursing homes feed funeral homes. "No visits."

Doctors and nurses, therapists, pharmacists

spend twelve-hour shifts, puzzled, they insist.
They've seen nothing like this; their patients are dying.
Despite their best efforts, whatever they're trying.

The epidemic is epic; the pandemic is a fact.
Experts mobilize, an all-out attack.
Hydroxychloroquine, Remdesivir, plasma, it varies,
ventilators, respirators, PPE–the jargon's vocabulary.

Essential workers only allowed to report
to open food stores, gas stations, post offices, of course.
Everyone else, nonessential, whose egos take a blow,
they're told to stay home, not important, you know.

Administrators, directors, bosses scramble.
New paradigm shift, there's no good example
to do business as usual when usual's disappeared.
New guidelines and protocols, remote work appears.

No parties, no classes, no meetings, no church.
Meanwhile, businesses, families are left in the lurch.
Twenty-four-seven, kids, moms, dads, all three
are prisoners at home, watching TV!

Innovation's sensation, remote learning begins.
We Zoom, Google, Skype, share computers, login.
Teachers make plans to instruct from their homes.
No textbooks, but somehow online, lessons will come.

Then Covenant Church LIVESTREAMS to our places.
We gather together with worship and praises.
Small groups learn to Zoom; they'll show us a way
to connect with each other, united we'll stay.

ISOLATION OLYMPICS, a closed group, begins
with tricks, games, and challenges, chances to win.
Babies to eighties and teens in between
show videos, selfies, and create their own scenes.

We plan skits, build towers, go on walks, plant flowers,
line dance, bake bread, blow bubbles, fill the hours.
Fold origami, learn ASL alpha-spell our full names,
act charades, dress as Bible heroes, play board games.

Show science, tell jokes, build a fort, use our heads,
recite Scripture, favorite verses, embed in our hearts.
Draw eyes on BANANAS, find a blindfold bandana,
sketch pictures without looking, send card to Grandma.

Let's pretend, do a dance, karaoke, have some fun.
Make up words, do a selfie, and be silly, just once.
Mom chides, "Children, come! Do the silly hair one!"
"WHATEVER YOU SAY, MOM! Check it off, that's done!"

Church friends have such talent, amazing their wit!
Scholarly, accomplished, funny, and fit,
we've learned from each other, engineering, technology,
ballet, sculpture, artwork, writing, theology.

Rube Goldberged, stacked to the ceiling, read a book,
built forts, solved puzzles, jumped rope, learned a sport.
You gave us some fun when we were feeling so glum,
we're thankful to see videos, keeping up with each one.

We strengthened our families, accomplished so much:
brotherhood, fellowship, friendship, and such.
Olympic memories brought us oh, so close,
that's the big thing we'll appreciate most.

We'll look back at sharing the riches and plenty
with our church's great family in 2020.
ISOLATION OLYMPICS, how wonderful it's been.

Someday, we'll hug MASKLESS and rejoice once again.

***

Who could have known, who could have imagined, that as I write this to submit in September, the start of yet another season, we would still be facing the effects of COVID-19? We have endured a summer of lockdowns, and now the frustration of being socially distant has helped evoke demonstrations of anger. Sparks of unrest and concern, worry, isolation, and depression have erupted into civil unrest and unyielding division. Whole industries and icons of society are threatened. Culture is changing before our very eyes.

Although I continue to pray for peace, serenity, and continued problem-solving, my year's theme of Sharing the Plenty in 2020 could never have predicted storms, fires, earthquakes, riots in the streets, and the ravages of disease. Perhaps Mr. Rogers' mother was right. We need to look for the good in every situation, the helpers, the encouragers, the empathizers.

Indeed, there have been innovations in conducting business, in educating our children, in people's creativity, and certainly medical miracles that have occurred as scientists faced this crisis. And our church is flourishing because of activities like the one.

Conspiracy theories and politics aside, we'll leave it to history's pundits to pontificate. But Isolation Olympics would not have occurred without this time of crisis, and I'm personally thankful for it and this opportunity to share this story.

About the Author

Betty Whitaker Jackson writes Christian fiction, nonfiction, poetry, children's books, memoirs, and devotional guides. A career language arts teacher, she retired to Palm Bay, Florida where she now concentrates on writing and volunteering at Covenant Presbyterian Church and the Space Coast Symphony Orchestra. Her children, Paul and Nancy, and daughter-in-love, Mary, are members of the Orchestra, and her grandchildren are the inspiration for her two fundraising books for the Orchestra, *Yay! Hooray! It's Concert Day!* and *I Hear Music Everywhere*. In the last eight years, she has published 24 books, and blogs regularly at https://www.bettyjackson.net. She won

First Prize in the *LifeRich Reader's Digest Memoir* Writing Contest and is published in eleven juried anthologies. She thanks Space Coast Writers' Guild for its encouragement.

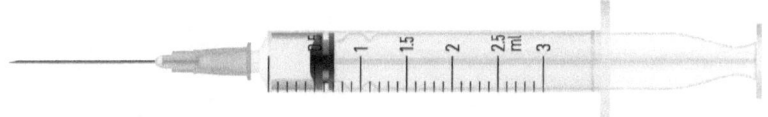

PANDEMIC

Protesters at the Unite for Freedom rally, where thousands gathered in Trafalgar Square, London on August 29, 2020 to hear calls for lockdown rules to be removed. (JessicaGirvan / Shutterstock.com)

As the pandemic wore on, people became fatigued and increasingly irate at the limitations on their lives, from store closures to wearing masks in public to bans on private gatherings. The sweeping powers of government became very apparent in the health crisis.

PANDEMIC

"Current evidence doesn't support public needing masks."

Theresa Tam, Chief Public Health Officer of Canada.
March 30, 2020

"Wear a mask in closed spaces, crowded places and where distancing is difficult."

Theresa Tam, Chief Public Health Officer of Canada.
October 12, 2020

WHAT NEW NORMAL?

Nicholas Kaplan

Cosmo and Hazel survived a cancer scare, heart problems, an airplane crash, and a still remembered (if somewhat humorously) boating accident. They both worked all their lives with an "honest day's labor" philosophy, paid their taxes, and gave away some of their money toward compassionate causes.

Their attitude towards life was uplifting, balanced, and vociferous only when they witnessed cruelty and injustice towards man or animal. Never were they arrested for any crime or spent a night in jail. They were sociable but not influential and voted in the land of the free and home of the brave. For the most part, they were smack in the middle of any demographic you could conjure up. No, they were neither saints nor sinners, flag wavers nor flag burners.

Both were born and lived in the North with all of its hurriedness and misgivings. By the grace of God, they avoided street thugs and gangsters, surviving to live a life which they considered normal.

***

Standing outside of their home, they see almost no one. No children are playing or going to and from school. No old folk, middle-aged folk, or young folk. Occasionally the slight glimpse of a courageous delivery driver dropping off a purchase to the house across the street. Cosmo mumbles, "That's where all the dammed toilet paper is going, I just know it."

The sky is still sunny and bright and remarkably haze-free, with more birds vocalizing and flittering than ever. Hazel, hoping that her mate could brighten up her lingering premonitions, remarked, "For the first time, I could clearly hear the wind whooshing through the picket fences and the drone of a small aircraft overhead." Cosmo, entering from an adjacent room, speaks with a booming voice, "I hear that gasoline is selling at a very low price, but no one can go anywhere or do anything without fear." Both of their observations amounted to rhetorical statements.

***

Activating their forty-seven-inch monolithic, HD certified, five-millimeter-thick, smarter than smart television screen, they hear and see the Doctors, an array of Government spokespeople, and the news of the day and always, the count. The dead and infected have been marginalized only to be supplanted with incessant attorney commercials on how to get outrageous payments, an ever-increasing desperate display of brashness, and other pitches. The media reporting is punctuated with auto insurance companies gesturing to give money back to people, and not to be forgotten, a newsworthy "crape skin creme" testimonial.

One of their children, whom they last saw and hugged three years ago, asked them through an email how they felt about their "bunker" existence. Cosmo wanted to tell them about his Grandfather, who survived the last tuberculosis outbreak, two World Wars, unemployment during the Great Depression, and all the other calamities of extreme weather and the like, but unsarcastically chose not to. "Chill out and relax," he typed back in response.

Hazel, after witnessing what Cosmo had written, let go a torrent of built-up emotions at him. "When I worked as a nurse practitioner, I was so tired and worn out from my shift, I couldn't remember where I lived. Twelve and sixteen hours a stretch performing with sickness all around is very taxing on the soul and body. You become somewhat numb to the pleas and cries for help, and sometimes, you don't want to know if they make it or not. People are already congratulating themselves for nothing and telling us, "were all in this together." It's all a bunch of garbage. That's just something people say to make themselves feel important. It's like a courtesy, you know, "Come visit us any time."

With all humility and candor, Hazel and Cosmo likened their new existence to being admitted to a giant hospital, awaiting test results, and hoping and praying for the best. Sitting in front of the computer with his normally compassionate wife nearby, Cosmo faces her and says, "Honey, since they keep saying we're all in this together, what if this Earth has become God's waiting room? I'm glad we are waiting together." Hazel quips back, "That's nice dear, but now what should we do with the body in the freezer?"

About the Author

Nicholas Kaplan is a first-time author living in Florida. Since the 1960's, he worked and traveled throughout

Europe and the Middle East. Now retired, he has written articles and essays for the Brevard Scribblers anthology *Driftwood*, and is a member of the Space Coast Writers' Guild. His self-published novel (under the *nom de plume* of Nicholas Taylor) entitled *The Long Game* is a 21st century story about espionage and government corruption, and is available on Amazon.

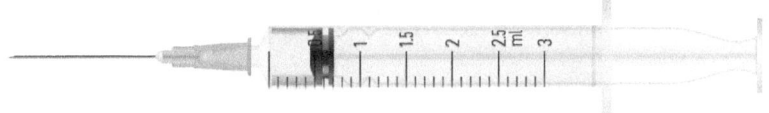

NO ENTRY
WITHOUT FACE MASK

Perhaps no other item of "personal protective equipment" (PPE) was more controversial than face masks. At the start of the pandemic, the public was told not to wear masks, partly due to a shortage of them; they were reserved for healthcare workers. A few months later, agencies like the CDC advised everyone to wear a mask, and some state and local governments made it mandatory. (Kagan Kaya / Shutterstock.com)

PANDEMIC

"We are in an unprecedented global pandemic that ... really sucks."

Prime Minister Justin Trudeau. October 27, 2020.

DEALING WITH DISAPPOINTMENT

Ashley McGrath

The events of this year were not part of the vision I had for 2020 on January 1. I didn't think COVID-19 would affect my life much as long as I didn't contract it. WHO declared the coronavirus a "public health emergency of international concern" on January 30. This worried my parents and me a bit because we had planned to go on a Western Caribbean cruise with my dad's family the first week of March. The cruise was to disembark from Miami; there was a huge spike in COVID-19 cases in Miami-Dade County early in the pandemic.

My parents and I decided to proceed with the cruise, which was terrific. Everywhere we went on the ship, there was an employee dispensing hand sanitizer; this did not happen during our previous cruises. On March 11 (three days after our return), WHO declared COVID-19 a pandemic. Not long after that, scheduled cruises were canceled. I'm glad we had this family vacation. None of my relatives came down with the virus, and we had so much fun before our lives were restricted.

Florida Governor Ron DeSantis ordered bars to be closed by 5:00 P.M. on March 17 – St. Patrick's Day of all days! (Ironically, I was playing free poker, but not drinking, with friends at a bar when this happened.) Three days later, inside dining at restaurants wasn't allowed, so the poker league I participated in was forced to close. Churches were also closed, which shocked me. Going to church was a weekly routine for my parents and me all my life. We began observing Mass live-streamed on YouTube, making us feel somewhat connected to our church. However, it wasn't the same as physically going to church and seeing our friends. My mom and I squeezed in an enjoyable visit to the Brevard Zoo before it closed in late March.

When April 1 came around, I'd hoped the pandemic was an elaborate April Fools' Day hoax. Alas, it wasn't; as a matter of fact, Governor DeSantis issued a stay-at-home order that went into effect by the end of that week. Five days later it was my birthday. Instead of going out to my favorite restaurant Olive Garden for dinner, my parents and I had takeout from a nearby pizzeria and store-bought chocolate cake for dessert. Around that time, I was assigned a new client for my work-from-home call monitoring job, so I was scheduled for training. I received a stimulus check, which was a nice bonus that paid for my new work laptop. I kept in touch with some of my relatives from

New York through video calls. Seeing their faces made it easier for me to cope with being unable to visit them in the foreseeable future.

At the beginning of May, my parents and I ventured out to the sunflower maze at Sledd's U-Pick Farm in Mims. Excited to get out of the house, I was amazed by the beauty of what appeared to be endless rows of sunflowers. I started having doctor's appointments through video chats; I enjoyed seeing doctors from the comfort of my home. On May 12 (two days after Mother's Day), I had myself tested for COVID-19 out of curiosity. Having a long Q-Tip shoved up my nose was unpleasant, but thankfully, the test results came back negative. Shortly after that, Florida began to reopen, so I could go back to church and poker, but as a person with health issues, I had to take some precautions. Every time I left my house, I wore a face mask, used a hand sanitizer frequently, and didn't touch anyone.

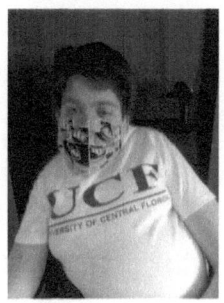

In June, I was pleasantly surprised when the Space

Coast UCF Alumni Chapter informed me that I was selected to be the recipient of its Notable Knight Award. I will receive the award at an event in the future. I volunteered at a writers' conference that was originally scheduled for late April. The woman who ran the conference gave me an aloe plant as a token of her appreciation. There was something comforting about keeping a plant alive while I kept hearing about COVID-19 deaths. My mom and I took my dad to a pub to which we'd never been for a delectable lunch on Father's Day. It was quiet because we were the only customers eating indoors at that time.

Unfortunately, Florida's COVID-19 rate kept increasing significantly after its reopening. Because of coronavirus interstate travel restrictions, I was unable to attend a cousin's wedding and my maternal grandmother's burial (both planned a year in advance) in New York in August. A few of my poker friends contracted COVID-19 during the summer. So, I took a break from poker for the first half of September to prevent exposing my mom, who was scheduled to have surgery in the middle of the month.

For me, the year 2020 has been an extended exercise in dealing with disappointment. Despite this, I know I have a lot for which to be thankful. I didn't contract the coronavirus. None of my relatives or friends died from it. I didn't lose my job, and I'm not struggling financially. With my parents, I have a decent home in which to quarantine myself. We were fortunate the pandemic resulted in only an inconvenience for us. Along with following CDC guidelines, we all need to maintain a positive attitude for the duration of the pandemic.

About the Author

Ashley McGrath is a quality analyst for a call monitoring company. A lifelong Brevard County resident, Ashley has a master's degree in Applied Sociology from UCF. In 2014, she published her autobiography *UnabASHed by Disability* (available on Amazon). Her writing has also appeared in a local bilingual newspaper, online columns, and eight other anthologies. A former treasurer of the Space Coast Writers' Guild, Ashley is the coordinator of its Don Argo Award Florida-based writing contest.

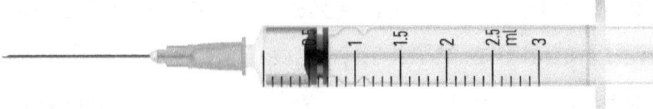

PANDEMIC

The COVID-19 pandemic caused widespread school closures. Education systems from K-12 to universities were forced to pivot to online learning very quickly. For many students, learning from home, using a computer instead of a teacher, was not a positive experience. It was also difficult for parents, who scrambled to find daycare for their children, and to become educators themselves. (Sam Wordley / Shutterstock.com)

PANDEMIC

"President Vladimir Putin said that Russian authorities had the coronavirus crisis under full control and that everything would work out with God's help, even as the country on Sunday registered a record daily rise in cases of the new virus."

Andrew Osborn and Polina Devitt, Reuters. April 19, 2020.

THE 1918 SPANISH FLU IN BREVARD

Rick Neale

The material in this chapter is © FLORIDA TODAY and originally appeared in the newspaper on August 13, 2020 under the headline "1918 Spanish flu shuttered schools, killed young and old alike across Brevard County." It is reproduced here with permission.

Brevard County was a sparsely settled, mosquito-plagued frontier when the Spanish flu pandemic swept the nation more than a century ago, wreaking havoc in metropolitan areas. But much like COVID-19, the influenza still shuttered schools, closed churches and triggered quarantines in October 1918 in Brevard's biggest cities, Cocoa (population 1,400+) and Titusville (population 1,300+).

And sadly, Mrs. John Eberwine of Artesia – a long-lost Banana River village near today's Port Canaveral – lost three sons to the dread virus. They "answered the last roll call" while preparing to fight for the U.S. Army in World War I, the Cocoa Tribune reported on Nov. 7, 1918.

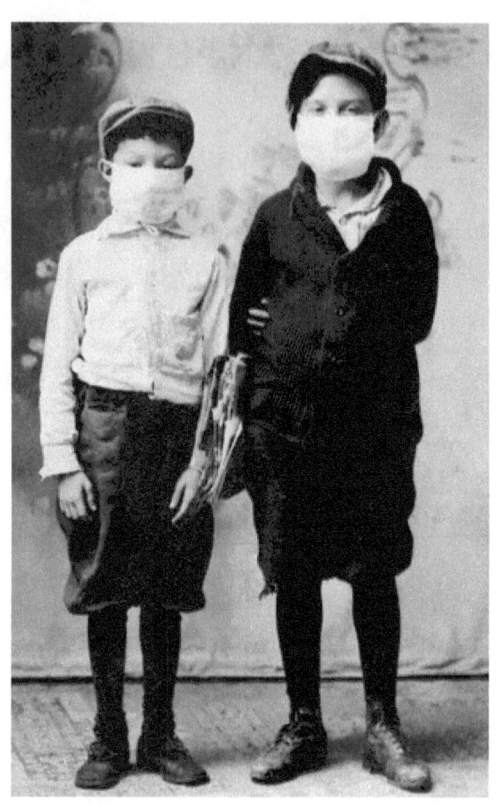

Don Hoover and Joe Sistrunk of Starke, Florida, ready for school during the 1918 Spanish flu epidemic. (Florida Memory/State Archives)

Her first son, Charles, died in May 1918 following an attack of pneumonia at Camp Jackson, South Carolina. Then in October, son Fritz died of the same disease at the same camp. The third son, George, died the next day while aboard a troop transport ship bound for France.

"The great difference, as most of us know, is how

many more of the young people were affected by the Spanish influenza," said Gordon Patterson, a professor and historian at the Florida Institute of Technology. "And that was brought home in, I thought, the really terrible story of the mother who lost three sons to the disease," Patterson said.

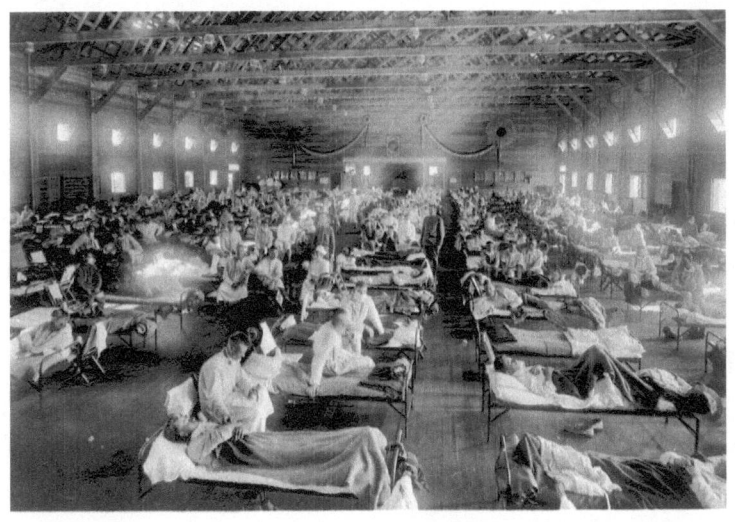

Influenza victims crowd into an emergency hospital near Fort Riley, Kansas in this 1918 file photo. (AP Photo/National Museum of Health)

The 1918 influenza pandemic ranks as the worst in modern history, killing at least 50 million worldwide and about 675,000 in the U.S., the Centers for Disease Control and Prevention reports.

Microfilm copies of two weekly newspapers, the

Cocoa Tribune and the long-titled East Coast Advocate and Indian River Chronicle in Titusville, offer a rare glimpse of local Spanish influenza disruptions. Copies of the Melbourne Times, a third publication, are no longer available from that era, said Michael Boonstra, genealogy librarian at the Central Brevard Library in Cocoa.

Booming during the Progressive Era, rural Brevard County's census population skyrocketed 80% between 1910 and 1920 – from 4,717 people to 8,505. The fishing villages of Melbourne and Eau Gallie each boasted 500-odd residents. WWI savings stamps were purchased by residents of long-vanished Brevard communities: Hopkins, Tillman, Courtenay, Allenhurst, Shiloh, Pineda, Indianola, Georgiana, Lotus, Aurantia, Banyan, Tropic, and Bonaventure.

Steamboats and railroad transport made Cocoa a bustling port for the citrus industry. Paved streets for automobiles had just been introduced. A newspaper article chronicled the excitement when residents spotted "three hydro-aeroplanes" flying along the riverfront.

And Cocoa Ice & Light Co. advertised a newfangled innovation: "Get Your House Wired: Electricity is Cheaper than Gas or Oil."

"Back in 1918, it would have been a bigger deal to travel from town to town. If you drive on U.S. 1 today, a lot of the towns blend together. But Cocoa was very different and very far away from Titusville, Eau Gallie and Melbourne," said Ben Brotemarkle, executive director of the Florida Historical Society.

To journey from Cocoa to Titusville, for example, Brotemarkle said many residents preferred to travel via boat: "You would have to dedicate a whole day to the project."

On Oct. 8, 1918, to curtail the spread of Spanish influenza, Titusville officials ordered the closing of the public school, churches, Sunday school, the "moving picture show" and all places of public gathering.

Four days later, Cocoa Mayor William A. Heaton issued a similar proclamation.

"He basically put the town in lockdown, canceling all public gatherings. That seemed to be a prudent response. He certainly took decisive action," Brotemarkle said.

State health officials told Florida flu sufferers to quarantine – and their homes were marked with placards to warn their neighbors.

PROCLAMATION.

In view of the prevalence of Spanish Influenza at this time, until further ordered, all Churches, Sunday Schools, Public schools, public gatherings and assemblies of all kinds, including lodges, secret societies, etc., are forbidden to be held or meet. And it is further ordered that any and all regulations as prescribed by Dr. W. R. Lincoln, City Health Physician, shall be carried out to the letter. Fail not under penalty.

Witness my official signature and the corporate seal of said City of Cocoa, this October 12, 1918.   WM. A. HEATON,
Attest: Mayor.
  A. L. BRUNER, Clerk.

Cocoa Mayor William A. Heaton issued a Spanish influenza closure proclamation on Oct. 12, 1918. (Cocoa Tribune)

What's more, children were forbidden from returning to school for seven days after a physician pronounced him or her cured.

"Some of the similarities are interesting in that the schools were closed, public meetings and gatherings were banned in most places, they recognized that coughing and sneezing could spread it – and all this just over a hundred years ago from today," Boonstra said. – and

Brevard fared better than Miami, where the city's hospital was overwhelmed by ill troops from Naval Air Station Dinner Key. More than 400 residents died from Spanish flu in Jacksonville in October 1918 – and that sum may not have included 155 dead at the predecessor of Naval Air Station Jacksonville, the Florida Times-Union reported.

Cocoa's Red Star Pharmacy ran newspaper ads during the 1918 Spanish influenza pandemic touting "sanitary paper cups" at its new fountain. (Cocoa Tribune)

Patterson noted a list of highlights from the 1918 Cocoa-Titusville newspaper clippings:

Spanish flu severely struck more young people than COVID-19

"Sunday evening, at eight o'clock, the Death Angel came to the home of Mr. and Mrs. Allan A. Sapp, and claimed their precious little 14 months' old baby girl, that had suffered for more than two weeks with Spanish influenza, which was followed by pneumonia."

That November 1918 East Coast Advocate and Indian River Chronicle story – headlined "Death of an Infant" – relayed the fate of little Marguerite Katherine Sapp, who was laid to rest in the Titusville Cemetery.

Patterson was also struck by the death of Eau Gallie resident LeLand V. McMillan, who died at age 28 of complications following influenza. His brother had died a few weeks earlier at a military training camp.

"There were obituaries for infants all the way up to older folks, and all people in between. There were people in their 20s," Brotemarkle said.

The 1918 pandemic occurred during World War I

A cartoon advertisement offered a wartime warning: "Coughs and Sneezes Spread Diseases: As Dangerous as Poison Gas Shells."

"The Spanish influenza occurred in the midst of a world war. And so, the way in which it was thought about was, this is something that poses an existential threat – just as the war posed an existential threat to the doughboys that went," Patterson said.

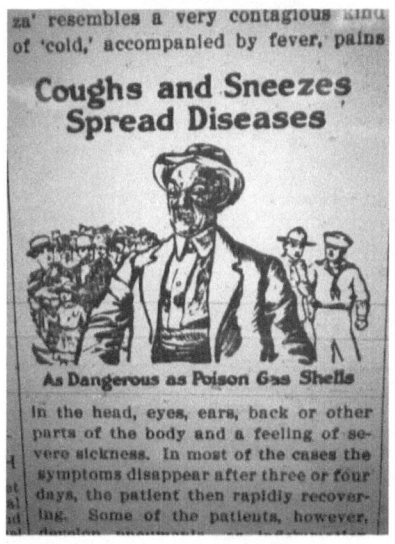

za' resembles a very contagious kind of 'cold,' accompanied by fever, pains

Coughs and Sneezes Spread Diseases

As Dangerous as Poison Gas Shells

In the head, eyes, ears, back or other parts of the body and a feeling of severe sickness. In most of the cases the symptoms disappear after three or four days, the patient then rapidly recovering. Some of the patients, however,

This World War I-inspired Spanish flu cartoon ran in the Oct. 18, 1918 edition of the East Coast Advocate and Indian River Chronicle in Titusville. (East Coast Advocate and Indian River Chronicle)

"I wonder if that is one of the differences between 1918-19 and 2020. The full gravity of this existential threat has not, to a substantial number of people, become current," he said.

"It is something that the 18- or 19-year-old in South Beach or at the end of Fifth Avenue says, 'Oh, I'm not worried about it for myself.' But the consequence of that is that the disease can spread into populations which are immunocompromised, or at high risk," he said.

This undated photo shows a Georgia Tech home game during the 1918 college football season, with fans wearing masks in the stands as the Spanish flu pandemic struck the United States in two waves. (Thomas Carter via AP)

Spanish flu claimed the son of Eau Gallie's founder

In 1870, William H. Gleason bought 16,000 acres and named the area Eau Gallie. He was Florida's first elected lieutenant governor, and his Queen Anne-styled home on Pineapple Avenue is listed on the National Register of Historic Places.

His son, Capt. G.G. Gleason, succumbed to Spanish flu-related pneumonia in 1918 in St. Augustine at age 53. He previously lived in Eau Gallie, where he worked as superintendent of Indian River Steamers.

G.G. Gleason's nephew, William Lansing Gleason, would later co-found Indian Harbour Beach. Lansing Island and Florida Tech's 480-seat W. Lansing Gleason Performing Arts Center are named in his honor.

Medical quackery: Laxative touted as virus fighter

A lengthy advertisement touted Tanlac, a "powerful reconstructive tonic" that supposedly fortified the weak and tired against deadly Spanish influenza. Tanlac was sold in Titusville at Banner Drug Store.

"In connection with the Tanlac treatment, it is necessary to keep the bowels open by taking Tanlac Laxative Tablets, samples of which are included with every bottle of Tanlac," the advertisement said.

Tanlac – which contained 17% alcohol – was denounced by the Journal of the American Medical Association as a fraudulent medicine of the vaudeville variety that had "doubtless relieved the people of the South of many thousands of dollars."

Patterson drew parallels with the Bradenton church that sold a toxic bleach-based "miracle mineral solution" as a coronavirus treatment. Last month, federal prosecutors charged four men in the scheme –

one of whom wrote President Donald Trump a letter touting chlorine dioxide as an alleged COVID-19 cure.

"My God, it makes me think all bad ideas come from Florida," Patterson said, laughing.

Members of the St. Louis Red Cross Motor Corps stand on duty during the influenza epidemic on Oct. 10, 1918. (Library of Congress)

Woman becomes trailblazing tax assessor

Brevard County Tax Assessor Willard Hall, 47, who was born in Sharpes, fell ill after his family contracted the disease during a trip to Jacksonville.

They returned home to Titusville, where Hall took to his bed and died within about a week.

"Many hearts were plunged into deep grief," the

Cocoa Tribune reported

Gov. Sidney Catts appointed his wife, Frances, to fulfill his unexpired term in office. This marked the first time in Florida history that a woman was appointed to fill such a county office, the East Coast Advocate and Indian River Chronicle reported.

Like today, health care workers on the front lines

Cocoa native Alberta Battle died at age 28, the Cocoa Tribune reported.

"By profession she was a trained nurse, a graduate of the East Coast hospital in St. Augustine, and during the influenza epidemic she nursed her husband through an attack of the disease," the newspaper reported.

"Not strong herself, she, too, became a victim of the disease, which later developed into pneumonia she was unable to successfully carry through the fight to throw it off."

She was survived by her husband – and their 7-week-old infant daughter.

About the Author

Rick Neale is the South Brevard Watchdog Reporter at FLORIDA TODAY, where he has worked since 2004. A former USA Today correspondent, the Melbourne resident previously reported in Ohio for the Port Clinton News Herald and Fremont News-Messenger. He helped FLORIDA TODAY win first place in breaking news in the 2019 Florida Society of News Editors contest by covering Hurricane Michael from a Panama City hotel that suffered extensive damages during the Category 5 storm.

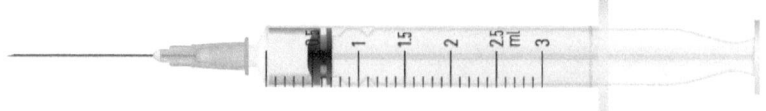

PANDEMIC

Forced closures of many businesses led to empty downtowns. Most people worked from home (if they could), or simply lost their jobs. This is a view of Manhattan in New York City on May 7, 2020. (tetiana.photographer / Shutterstock.com)

PANDEMIC

Gov. Ron DeSantis said Sunday the state remains on the right track in its response to the coronavirus outbreak despite a mounting number of new cases.

"If you follow the guidelines, you're fine," he said while speaking at Ascension Sacred Heart Hospital in Pensacola. "We have Universal Studios, they have this great safety plan, and they have the different things — [requiring a] mask, all this other stuff — [and] they've done a great job. They haven't had any problems. And it doesn't take a lot, you've just got to be careful."

His comments came as Florida reported 8,530 new coronavirus positive tests on Sunday, a day after the state set a record for a single-day increase with Saturday's 9,585 reported cases. The second highest day was Friday, with 8,942.

The state's death toll was 3,419, up 29 from the day before.

Steven Lemongello, Orlando Sentinel. June 28, 2020

THE CORONAVIRUS IN MELBOURNE

Rick Neale

Quarantined, he peered through the window at the trio of twinkling lights beyond the river in Indialantic, wondering how they were still shining in the darkness.

"Shelter in place," the experts said. After dumping one of Ethel Raymond's cans of Campbell's chicken noodle soup into a bowl, he settled into her creaky recliner. He studied the distant beachside lights past her ruffled curtains, watching for signs of activity. Did they have generators?

He hadn't dared set foot outdoors in months.

Downtown Melbourne lost power soon after the vaccinated carriers changed. Hundreds of bullet casings – now mostly obscured by fallen leaves and browned palm fronds – still littered New Haven Avenue, left by the Florida Army National Guard soldiers pushing westward from U.S. 1, fighting to reach the airport.

The roaring fire sparked by the soldiers gutted a

good percentage of the businesses east of Matt's Casbah, and the landmark 1900 Building collapsed upon itself after flames incinerated the roof. Black acrid smoke was still billowing when he sprinted into the Trinity Towers East lobby. Scrambling, he shoved sofas and loveseats to barricade the glass entry doors and hid in the stairwell for safety, trembling and crying, listening to gunfire and screaming.

The 14-story senior housing complex had been his silent home ever since. Fortunately, food remained plentiful: Trinity Towers East housed 156 apartments, and the taller Trinity Towers West loomed next door. If his provisions ran out before he was rescued, he could try raiding Ember & Oak or Mainstreet Pub or La Crepe down the block ... they stored canned foods on their restaurant shelves, right?

But the Trinity Towers were an easier source. Populated by residents age 62 and older – some of whom were physically disabled – they had posed a manageable physical threat, all things considered. The complex must have been largely evacuated during the initial chaos. Any vaccinated remaining on the lower floors surely must have starved to death by now, he reasoned. It turns out they weren't good with doors or with stairs.

He had to kill three to reach and secure Floor 14 that first day, including Ethel, but he later cleared nearby Floors 13 and 12 with minimal incident. He felt fortunate and secure, all things considered, with plenty more apartments to plunder in a similar fashion.

Fortunate? He settled back in Ethel's flower-print recliner, tilted his head back, and closed his eyes.

What sort of skeletally pathetic existence was this? Cooped up in this empty building, alone, night after pitch-black night?

Just don't think about the past.

Every night after sunset, he religiously roamed windows across vacant Floor 14, looking for lights from the tower's tallest vantage point. On the northern horizon, Patrick Air Force Base perpetually emitted a white glow in the darkness, like a distant metropolis. He had spotted military aircraft landing and taking flight since the day he arrived, traveling to and from unknown points to the north. Where were they flying? Who was operating the base?

Could they ever find him?

Far to the west, he saw small clusters of lights every

night glowing miles away, beyond the airport and Melbourne Square Mall, closer to Interstate 95. Out of the question; he doubted he could even make it as far as Babcock Street.

To the south, nothing but treetops and darkness.

Patrick Air Force Base had to be his salvation. Ludicrous ideas crossed his mind throughout his dull, lonely, endless doldrum days: "Could I light a fire on the rooftop to attract their attention?"

But he never considered traveling there. The causeways were still barricaded to vehicle traffic, so far as he knew. And he would have no route of escape.

Russia's surprising Sputnik V coronavirus vaccine had proven every bit as shocking to the United States as its namesake satellite did back in 1957. With America's political system deadlocked in partisan polarization – and COVID-19 deaths outpacing the rest of the planet – Vladimir Putin's much-touted vaccine proved stunningly successful in clinical trials.

U.S. distribution was swift. With tens of millions of free vaccinations administered at schools, workplaces, churches, retailers, and nonprofits – month after month – cases had dwindled to a small fraction of the numbers seen during the opening 2020 days of the pandemic. Politicians eased social distancing restrictions, and the economy responded by rebounding near full strength.

Ironic how, in the early days, some cable-television talking heads had discussed America attaining "herd immunity," meaning the bulk of the population would eventually catch COVID-19, develop antibodies, medically recover, and become immune to future infection.

Herd immunity? The Russian vaccine created a herd: "The newly mutated virus appears to affect everybody who was vaccinated, and they are highly dangerous and highly contagious! Do not go outdoors! Shelter in place! Defend yourselves!" That's what Ethel's battery-backup clock radio had said before the last radio stations went off the air.

South Florida was the first area to fall, followed by Tampa-St. Petersburg, Orlando, Jacksonville. Why hadn't he fallen sick? What was happening across Melbourne, in Florida, America, the world? Was he somehow immune?

God knows his family wasn't.

Finishing his soup, he studied the lights in

Indialantic.

***

Influenza took hold days later.

He woke up abruptly that night suffering from body aches, cold sweat soaking the mattress of Ethel's perfume-smelling, brass-frame bed.

No!

He sat bolt upright, terrified, blood pressure rising. Was this happening? Pressing his hand against his clammy forehead, he knew he was running a fever.

Could he still taste? Could he still smell?

Scrambling out of bed, he stumbled to Ethel's bathroom. Hands trembling, he lit a candle and rummaged through her medicine cabinet and vanity, where he had stashed his stockpile of valuable medical goods taken from her former neighbors. He downed two Tylenols and grabbed a bottle of NyQuil for later.

A blurred haze, for days.

Delirious dreams about the Indialantic lights,

beckoning across the river, and finally meeting the people there. They were people he knew from high school, helpful strangers, old girlfriends, co-workers.

Dreams about talking with the deer and wild hogs he had seen grazing the overgrown landscaping along Strawbridge Avenue. Of vivid childhood memories: Little League baseball games, long-lost friends, his parents.

Coughing and congested with the flu, he was petrified he would develop pneumonia.

Days passed. He had long since lost track of conventional time. Alone with a dead phone and no electricity: hours, days, weeks, months. He had learned to watch the sun and create daily action plans according to daylight hours, like his ancestors thousands of years ago.

Watching them roving the streets below, hunched alone and in pairs and in packs – like chimpanzees? gorillas? baboons? – he doubted he could survive a mad dash to the Melbourne Causeway. Much less cross it.

Odd how they grabbed whatever objects were handy as primitive weapons. And how he had watched them occasionally turn on their weaker brethren: the old, the young, the injured.

Were they contagious?

They hunted him in his nightmares.

Finally, his fever broke. As days dragged by, subtly at first – noticeably before long – he recovered. The exhaustion subsided. His sinus woes faded away.

But how had he gotten sick? He was alone. The last time he had heard someone else, it was her piercing, frantic, gobbling screams echoing from the streets past the post office, pleading and crying for help.

***

He dropped the bowl of Hormel chili on Ethel's carpet, upside-down.

Two black HH-60G Pave Hawk helicopters were patrolling in tandem southward along the barrier island, their familiar rotary-engine-thumps reverberating across the quiet landscape.

Unbelievable! He leaped to his feet, stunned, and watched the helicopters pass the Eau Gallie Causeway, drawing closer amid the morning sunshine.

Darting to Ethel's front door, he grabbed his getaway supply backpack, strapped it onto his shoulders, and rushed back to her windows in disbelief.

The twin Pave Hawks banked slightly toward his direction as they reached Indialantic, then slowed, hovering and circling beyond the causeway. Were they looking for a landing site on Fifth Avenue? Or near the boardwalk?

Time to go!

After months of contemplating ridiculous, random escape scenarios, this was it.

His cards had been dealt. He had to reach those choppers. Now!

Nostalgia? He stumbled into Ethel's rickety recliner, sent her ceramic lamp flying, and didn't give her home – or his – a second thought while slamming the door on the way out.

Adrenaline and urgency propelled him down the stairwell, surging like a refreshing ocean wave as his feet pounded the steps, floor by floor.

Reaching the lobby, he flung aside the furniture,

pushed open the doors, and ran outside. He noticed the warm sea breeze, and the sunshine, and the humidity, and the brilliant blue sky.

Run! He sprinted full speed down Strawbridge Avenue, past the skeletons with bleached rib cages. He saw a Pave Hawk still aloft, beyond the left side of the One Harbor Place office tower. Was the other still circling?

Pop!

Did he hear that from his left ankle? Or did he feel it? Or both? He had rolled his ankle hopping over the sidewalk curb.

Limping, slowing, he hobbled past long-vacant Melbourne City Hall to the railroad tracks. The U.S. 1 intersection was dead ahead. Just beyond those abandoned vehicles was a downhill rush to the foot of the causeway – the bridge to Indialantic, where the Pave Hawks and the people with the lights could save him.

Surrounded, he panicked and screamed as the cannibals closed in.

About the Author

Rick Neale is the South Brevard Watchdog Reporter at FLORIDA TODAY, where he has worked since 2004. A former USA Today correspondent, the Melbourne resident previously reported in Ohio for the Port Clinton News Herald and Fremont News-Messenger. He helped FLORIDA TODAY win first place in breaking news in the 2019 Florida Society of News Editors contest by covering Hurricane Michael from a Panama City hotel that suffered extensive damages during the Category 5 storm.

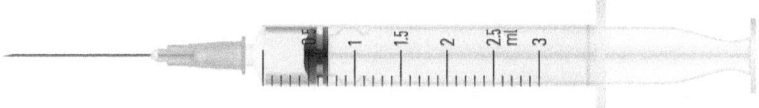

PANDEMIC

Cases

	Total ▾	🇺🇸 United States ▾	All regions ▾

Cases
13M
+103K

Deaths
263K
+1,178

Location	Cases ↓	Deaths
Texas	1.22M +4,504	21,709 +173
California	1.18M +8,988	19,025 +43
Florida	962K +0	18,253 +0

COVID-19 cases in the USA, as of November 27, 2020. America has the most cases of any country in the world, a stunning result for Earth's most advanced nation. Here in Florida, we peaked at 15,300 new cases on July 12, 2020. (Google)

PANDEMIC

"Five passengers aboard the first cruise ship to resume sailing in the Caribbean have tested positive for the coronavirus, according to reports and an interview with a passenger."

Will Feuer, CNBC. November 12, 2020.

A MOST UNUSUAL YEAR

Carolyn Newby

In March, my two sons, daughter, and daughter-in-law, treated me to dinner for my birthday. That was the last family outing that we were to experience from then, six months ago, through today and beyond. Nobody knows when the next will be.

It was our habit to gather for breakfast every Sunday morning, then go our separate ways. My destination was my church, where I've been a member for more than fifty years. Now it's no church as well as no breakfast.

Actually, I do have breakfast made by yours truly. Sometimes it's even a good breakfast, other times cereal or a slice of peanut butter toast before bringing up the computer for a live online service. This has relieved the strangeness somewhat. I get to see and hear our regular pastors and know which of my friends are attending with me by the "good mornings" and comments that we type in. The contemporary songs by the praise band inspire, but I can't sing them. I don't do such a great job with the traditional ones either, but I know how they're supposed to sound.

Right after the birthday dinner, all the businesses closed except for those deemed "essential." That meant the Friday night bowling league came to a screeching halt. We had already done away with the high fives and were bumping elbows instead. The season still had two months to go, and all of us had paid at least some money ahead. When things began to open up somewhat, the lanes manager called the league together for an emergency meeting to decide what should be done. The outcome was a cancelation of the rest of the season, money returned, and the prize fund split equally. Most of the members showed up wearing masks, but not all. This made me nervous, and I left as quickly as possible.

With the library closed, I was happy to hear that our Brevard Scribblers writers' club would try to meet live via Zoom. It is going very well, and I love hearing the readings and seeing all the familiar faces. The downside is not seeing the ones who do not have Zoom capability. Maybe we will eventually have a simultaneous Zoom and in-person meeting. Not being much of a tech-minded person, I'm not sure how that would work.

Going grocery shopping for the first time was quite an experience. Publix had initiated a senior hour when only senior citizens were allowed to enter the store. The hour was on Tuesday between 7:00 and 8:00 a.m. I donned my mask, thinking, "This is March. Why are they forcing all the old people to arrive here in the dark?" That wasn't the worst of it. The parking lot was full, the store was packed, and people were bumping carts into one another. The shelves where the paper products should be were completely bare. I was in total shock to see hand soap, sanitizer, cleaning products, canned food, and the meat counter nearly cleaned out. That was my last trip during the senior hour.

Now that most businesses are open again with new rules and safety procedures, I leave the house when absolutely necessary, armed with a mask and hand sanitizer. Upon arriving home, I lather up and wash my hands for the prescribed length of the Happy Birthday song. My hands have been washed so often that I no longer have fingerprints.

It is possible at this time to acquire toilet paper, napkins, and at least some cleaning products, though they may not be the preferred brand. Food is ample with usually at least one unexpected shortage. I've learned to be flexible.

The bank that I use has been closed for months. This morning I had an adventure. The ATM was out of cash, so I went to the one at Publix only to realize my debit card had not been returned. No way to get into the bank, so I drove a few miles to another branch that I had been told was functioning. That turned out to be true except that today is Wednesday, the one day it is closed. A lady with the same problem told me the branch across the Eau Gallie causeway should be open. This meant turning around, going back, and heading for the beach.

The bank was open, and I was able to get my cash. Then one of the executives told me the card could not be retrieved. It would be destroyed, and I would have to get a new one. She pulled up my account on her computer, entered all the information, issued a temporary card, and informed me that my new one would be coming by mail. All this before breakfast, which was about two hours late.

My team is bowling again in the new Fall league, but I am absent for the time being. I miss it so very much and want to see my long-time friends. But because of my age and a compromised immune system, I am in the high-risk category. I fail to see how eight people bowling side by side can keep a six-foot distance. Each week we bowl a different team as well, so the exposure level is relatively high. If no one gets sick, I would like to return eventually.

The church just last week returned to a schedule of one service only with many precautions. Seating is spaced, so the congregation sits far apart except for families, lots of sanitizing, no choir, and no passing of collection plates. No hymnals or bulletins. If it proves to be safe, I can handle the changes, but I plan to stick with the online service for a while.

Even my family, except for the one son who lives with me, has stayed away because of my status. I miss them. I miss my friends. I miss hugs. Thanksgiving dinner and Christmas together are not a given. It should be interesting to see what the rest of the year 2020 has in store for us. I'm not sure I want to know.

About the Author

Carolyn Newby is a resident of Eau Gallie in Melbourne, Florida. She writes poetry, short fiction, and nonfiction. She loves the First Church of Melbourne, family, the beach, gardening, and the Brevard Scribblers. Her other interests include reading, bowling, music, and Gator football. She was widowed after sixty years of marriage, which produced four children, five grandchildren, and ten great-grandchildren. She has published in thirty-seven of thirty-eight *Driftwood* anthologies.

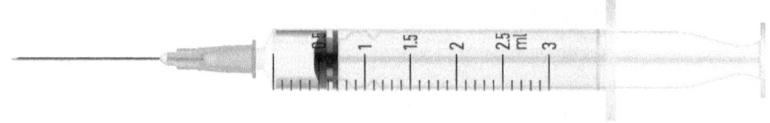

PANDEMIC

Cases

Total ▼   🌐 Worldwide ▼

Cases	Recovered	Deaths
61.1M	**39.2M**	**1.43M**

Location	Cases ↓	Recovered	Deaths
🇺🇸 United States	13M +103K	-	263K +1,178
🇮🇳 India	9.31M +44,489	8.72M	136K +524
🇧🇷 Brazil	6.2M +37,614	5.53M	171K +691
🇷🇺 Russia	2.22M +25,487	1.71M	38,558 +524
🇫🇷 France	2.18M +13,563	158K	50,957 +339

COVID-19 cases worldwide, as of November 27, 2020. These are the top five countries with the most infections. It's interesting that China is not listed. (Google)

PANDEMIC

"The degree of protective immunity conferred by infection with severe acute respiratory syndrome coronavirus 2 (SARS-CoV-2) is currently unknown. As such, the possibility of reinfection with SARS-CoV-2 is not well understood."

R. Tillett, J. Sevinsky, et al, The Lancet. October 12, 2020.

THE LIMINAL SPACE OF STILLNESS

Jamilette Pichardo

Death doesn't discriminate. That's something I learned very early in life. Death doesn't care about your sex, your religious beliefs, or how old you are. My name is Jayme. I'm not going to tell you that my name doesn't matter or that people don't matter. Because life does matter, and anyone on this planet can leave their mark on the world. It doesn't matter if you're a teacher, a lawyer, a doctor, or just a friend without a job. Everyone can leave a ripple effect by the people they touch and the things they do with their time.

I was born with Cerebral Palsy; it's a muscular condition that affects my body's lower extremities. Therefore, I use a wheelchair to move around independently. But more importantly, I was born with a compromised immune system. Ever since I was little, if anyone so much as sneezed or coughed on me, it would turn into some massive infection leading to hospitalization. I've lost track of how many times I've been hospitalized over something that should have been small throughout my very young life. I can't even pronounce half of the infections I've developed over the years.

When COVID-19 started to impact the world, the way I had to live my daily life changed drastically. For starters, even though I am disabled, I am very much a busybody. My mother calls me "alquitrán caliente," which means "hot tar" in Spanish. She gave me this nickname because I was hardly ever home. I was either working, at the library studying, out with friends and family, enjoying my time at the mall, or off seeing a movie. When COVID -19 hit, I couldn't do any of that. It wasn't even safe for me to ride the public bus, which was my only transportation source. I was confined to my house. My computer became my window to the world. The only other people I had to interact with were my mother and my cat. The isolation and the fear of contracting the virus was a living hell that seeped into my subconscious.

I have a younger brother who lives in Colorado. He moved there because he got a job offer working at a hospital that he couldn't refuse. My mom would cry a lot, worried about my brother. He told us that he did have a few patients who contracted the virus. Then while the virus was taking its toll, he decided to pay a visit to Florida. Personally, I thought he was crazy. But his decision for choosing to travel was because the plane tickets were super cheap. He figured if we were going to die because of this plague, at least he would have seen us one last time. I couldn't visit with my brother because he worked full-time at the hospital.

Ultimately, coming into contact with him would be detrimental to my health. I spoke to him from outside. He stood in my driveway as I looked through the window. But I mostly felt bad for my mother. He was her favorite child, and he had gone out of his way to see us. My mother couldn't even hug him out of fear of what it might do to me since he might be a carrier of the virus. I can say now without feeling embarrassed that I wondered if that would be the last time I would see my brother. I wished I could have hugged him and breathed in his scent one more time. I felt horrible that both he and my mom had to sacrifice their time together because of my stupid immune system and this virus. From then on, things just got worse.

***

For eight years, I have worked as a substitute teacher making ten dollars an hour. It wasn't much but with the little bit of disability money I received, plus what I made from substitute teaching, I could pay my bills and survive. With the epidemic, schools were shutting down and were asking people not to return to work. Even though I would be struggling financially, I was extremely relieved. I didn't have to choose between possibly dying every day if I decided to return to work. My mom wasn't working either, so financially, we were drowning. When you have to report to the government how much you're making monthly, they adjust your disability benefits. However, the system was really slow and tended to be two months behind on updating their information. As a result, even though I wasn't working, I was still receiving smaller payments from disability as if I were still working as a substitute teacher.

We had not yet been approved for food stamps, and my small disability amount went to paying our bills. We honestly didn't have money for food. We were drinking water from the tap and eating peanut butter and jelly sandwiches. It was the only thing that we could afford. The bread was our source of grain, and it was also filling our empty bellies. The peanut butter was our protein since we hadn't had meat or eggs in about two weeks. The jelly was our fruit and sugar. We were trying to hit as many food groups as possible. I was getting sick of peanut butter and jelly sandwiches. At one point, it was hard to look at the sandwich without gagging and forcing it down. But at least there was something in my stomach. There were nights when I had gone to bed hungry and irritable and wondering if there would be food for tomorrow. What I really wanted was a soda. My body was craving the caffeine and the energy boost.

I kept telling myself that we just had to get through these two months. I also prayed that our stimulus checks would arrive soon. Of course, they didn't. But God was good to me as I received help from an unexpected source. I had this friend who literally saved my mom and me from starving that month. Unbeknownst to me, my friend had gone out of their way to buy our groceries. We were so touched and happy when we received this blessing; we both started to cry. Someday I hope to pay that friend back.

Then my uncle came to visit. Here was the real kicker: he currently lives in New York – the capital of where the virus was taking life. My uncle was one of those people who didn't believe in the severity of this illness. He was one of those who thought people and the public were overreacting. He refused to stay isolated and wouldn't wear a mask. When he told my mom that he was first going to Puerto Rico to see my grandparents and then to Florida to see his daughter and us, my mom asked him if he was crazy. He would attend large block parties during the day and go to the clubs at night. He would call us gloating about everywhere he had been. Furthermore, he would state that this virus would not infringe on his daily life. It was his mantra. He was his own worst enemy and, by default, a hazardous threat to me.

The world as we knew it was shutting down. My uncle, on the other hand, continued to live his life as if nothing had changed. He enjoyed the once familiar pleasures of the beach. The air would smell of sea salt, food frying, and suntan lotion. I could imagine it all so clearly in my head. The large amounts of cars with numerous out-of-state license plates. They would accumulate and act like hot sardines packed across the scorching sand. People would mob the narrow boardwalk as they ran to look out into the shimmering water. It was a living cesspool for the virus to claim its next group of victims. I honestly wondered if he had a death wish. It was because of people like him that the virus was spreading so rapidly.

My mom told him that he couldn't come to stay at our house. He could only visit us by standing in my driveway and talking to each other through the window. My uncle told my mother and me that we were overreacting and to stop acting ridiculous. I reminded him that I had a compromised immune system and that having him visit could be dangerous. While he visited, he called every day. They're even came a point where I had to shut off my phone. He put so much pressure on me and my mom to see him. We said no repeatedly, and once again, he mentioned how we were overreacting and how ridiculous we sounded.

"Why would we sacrifice time with family over the fear of this virus?" my uncle asked. But he just didn't see things from my perspective, and once again, my mom was put in an uncomfortable and difficult situation because of me. I wasn't trying to sacrifice time or moments with my family. I wanted to see my family too. However, I didn't want my yearning for them to compromise their health. Why couldn't he understand that? More importantly, coming into contact with each other could ultimately cause all of us to run out of time. I just wanted all of us to survive this. For now, our survival would have to be enough.

However, for my uncle, survival wasn't enough. I couldn't believe he was willing to take the chance to travel to Puerto Rico to see my grandparents as well. They were both 84 years old, and my grandpa had underlying heart conditions and dementia. It seemed as if my uncle had no regard for anybody but himself. I thought that after his landlord had died from the virus it would have knocked some sense into him, and he would have taken this more seriously. It seemed to faze him only for a day, and then he was back to his daily routine. He always was exploring the city and ordering every day for breakfast plus lunch and dinner. I couldn't even remember the last time I had eaten out.

After he left, I was relieved, but then the isolation set

in. My mind was just racing. One night, I had a dream that I had contracted the virus. I was at a flea market with my grandma. This was something we had done many times when I was a child. The tradition continued through my teenage years. She loved to go to flea markets and antique shops. The dream was outside, and we were at a flea market. We were at a long rectangular plastic table as we were sorting pieces of driftwood. My grandma wore a straw sun hat embroidered with flowers in the center. I remember in the dream grandma had picked up a mahogany music box, and I had parked in front of her in my manual wheelchair.

"I have the Coronavirus," I told her. Suddenly and very violently, she started to cough up blood.

"I have the virus too, and I'm dying," my grandma said to me. This was all my fault. I had done this to her. Then her arms and legs fell off, and she was nothing but a torso asking me for my help. After the nightmare was over, I jolted awake in a cold sweat. I couldn't sleep for the rest of the night.

Another nightmare I had repeatedly was of having the virus and not being able to breathe. In reality, not being able to breathe was not something new to me. I was a pro at contracting respiratory infections. Most of the time, if not all the time, I had to be put on oxygen, unable to breathe independently. There were countless times in my life when doctors had to extract fluid from my lungs with a large needle. However, in the dream, I needed to be intubated, and I was begging them not to do it. I didn't want to be unable to talk. I had that dream time and time again.

***

When you're in a chair most of the time that's all people see – especially doctors. People and doctors alike tend to think that you don't know or understand what's going on. They tend to think you can't advocate for yourself. But my mental faculties work just fine. Not communicating to them about what I did and did not need was not an option.

Even in real life, it is hard to get doctors and nurses to listen to me. About a year ago, I was hospitalized for having pneumonia (surprise, surprise). The fluid had traveled behind my heart. I had paged the nurse because I had to pee. The lady wanted to stick a catheter in my lady business. Here's the thing, when you're in a chair, most people, doctors and nurses included, assume that the diagnosis is paralysis. I had to explain to the nice lady I have CP, I'm not paralyzed.

"I have full function of my bladder," I told the nurse. "I just need help getting to the toilet."

"You're very fortunate," she told me. Silently I agreed. "A bedpan might be quicker," she suggested.

"No, thank you," I said. "I can use the toilet."

"I'm already behind on my rounds tonight," the nurse held up the light pink bedpan.

"No," I said firmly. She sighed and set the bedpan down. "Can you bring in a Sara Stedy?" I asked.

"How do you know what a Sara Stedy is?" she asked.

"It makes my toilet transfers a lot easier," I told her.

A few moments later, she returned wheeling in a Sara Stedy. A Sara Stedy was a manual standing aid with wheels. It was designed to help patients to pull themselves up into a standing position. In addition, it can be used for transferring from one surface to another. It featured an innovative pivoting seat that provided the user with stability once they were standing. The standing device had a crossbar handle so that the user can pull themselves up onto the rolling platform and support themselves.

The nurse reluctantly brought the device in front of me. I stepped onto the light blue platform and pulled myself into a standing position. She sighed as she pushed me into the bathroom and positioned me directly in front of the toilet. I pulled the hospital gown up to my knees and sat on the cold toilet seat. After I was seated, I released the urine from my bladder.

"I guess you do have control of your bladder," the nurse commented.

"Yeah," I said dryly. I prayed every night that I wouldn't be hospitalized during this pandemic. If that happened, I knew that I would be condemned to death.

***

If I wasn't being tormented by my nightmares, the loneliness and the silence was starting to get to me. I felt like my room was the eye of a hurricane. I was in the center of it, with the chaos falling around me. Then I remembered in the eye of the hurricane there was only deafening silence and solitude. I learned too much of that could also be dangerous. Sometimes I would go into my mind and have conversations with the people I longed to see. I would have long conversations with my grandparents inside my head. I missed them so much. They were my two favorite people in the entire world. I hated myself for not being able to travel to see them.

Some mornings I would imagine my grandma and

grandpa at my kitchen table as I ate my bowl of cereal. I would imagine my grandma sipping her Bustelo coffee and my grandpa reading the paper. Unlike me, my mother was a late sleeper, and she also struggled with depression. She wasn't much of a talker either and slept almost too much. As a result, my only companion aside from the TV and my cat was the silence.

Thus, I created imaginary grandma and grandpa to keep me company. My grandma was a beautiful woman with high cheekbones. She did not look like a grandma. She had ivory silk skin and long jet-black hair that fell to her shoulders. She had blunt bangs and chocolate almond-shaped eyes. She would disapprove of the cold cereal. Instead, she would make Avena de maíz, which is Spanish for hot porridge made from cornmeal sprinkled with cinnamon.

"What are your plans for today, Mamita?" Grandma asked. I would tell her about the latest piece of writing I was working on or what book I was currently reading. She never really approved of the kissing vampire ones.

"What about you, abuelita?" I wondered. She would tell me about all her friends at church and the latest gossip she had heard about certain celebrities.

"What are your ambitions for the future?" my

grandpa interjected. My grandpa was a short and stocky man. His dark hair had turned to gray, and he was completely bald at the top of his head. His eyes had turned completely light blue from cataracts. Like me, he used a wheelchair now to get around. Because of the wheelchairs, we had to coordinate our hugs. We had to align the wheelchairs just right to reach one another.

My grandpa was, and still is, my knight in shining armor. He taught me everything I know. In reality, he's more like my father. I never knew my biological father. But having Grandpa as my dad, not knowing my biological father didn't matter. Grandpa was more than enough. He taught me how to balance a checkbook and the importance of learning English and Spanish. Grandpa emphasized the importance of education, dedication, and hard work. He instilled in me that family was everything. He taught me the value of working hard and what it meant to put money away for the future. When he was officially diagnosed with dementia, I started to resent the world. He didn't deserve such a cruel fate. Subsequently, even though he was still with me, I felt like I was losing pieces of him. Some days he didn't even know who I was. But in my mind, I didn't have to include the dementia, the horrible sickness that was taking him away from me. There was only him and I and how we used to be.

"When do you plan to refocus on school and possibly getting your master's degree?" imaginary Grandpa asked.

"When I have the money and the proper writing portfolio," I replied.

"Don't get too serious with some boy," imaginary grandpa chided as he looked over the newspaper.

"I won't," I promised. The way my luck went, if I even kissed a guy, I could contract enough germs to catch pneumonia.

"You need to focus on your education and your future career first," imaginary grandpa insisted.

"Si, yo se," I told him. In my head, I would tell him not to worry, that eventually, things might go back to normal. But I knew I was lying to myself even if these were fake conversations living inside my head.

In my heart, I knew that I was letting him down. I had become complacent. He would want me to conquer the world – not hide from it. Thus, my main focus became staying alive and my writing. Consequently, to do that, I had to remain alone in my dominion of isolation. As I read and wrote, I was haunted by the echoes of people I wanted to be with, along with my memories of the people I loved.

There wasn't much that I could control in my life. Not even having the ability to walk or run. Yet, I wasn't standing still; I was lying in wait, fighting to survive. What I could control was my grit and attitude. I was a fighter. My whole life could attest to that. Death would not be my central narrative. I was given the gift of having more opportunities by my grandpa, and I was given a chance to live again and again by a higher power. I did not want to waste it.

Although living my life was massively different right now, I didn't want to limit myself. I didn't want to throw away my shot. My grandpa came over from Puerto Rico to New York when he was just eighteen years old. He didn't even have a high school diploma or speak English. But he didn't let that stop him. He had a dream of becoming a police officer. He knew that to do that, he would have to obtain a high school diploma. English was not his first language, but he did not let that be an obstacle that affected his ambitions. As a result, he took classes that taught him how to speak the English language. In addition, he built lamps in a factory, and at night he took courses to acquire his high school diploma. He graduated and then completed his training at the police academy. His next dream was that he would eventually build and own his own home. Later, he met my Mima, and they had four children. This included my three uncles and my mother. After thirty years on the police force, my grandpa retired and returned to Puerto Rico. He wanted to help his other family members who were struggling to rebuild their homes because of natural disasters that had hit the island.

When my grandparents arrived back in Puerto Rico my grandpa had another life mission that he wanted to fulfill. As a result, my abuelito made an investment for his entire family. He brought thirty acres of land and distributed it between his brothers and sisters. Meanwhile, my grandpa began to design and build a two-story house for his wife and children from the ground up. Eventually, that house became a reality. Brick by brick and cent by cent, he built his dream home for himself and my grandmother to grow old in together.

Thus, I figured if he could overcome all that, I could learn how to adapt and survive through this pandemic. I would not throw away my shot at living or thriving. I would not squander all the values that he had instilled in me. I would make something of my life despite my compromised immune system and disability. So, I read every book that I could get my hands on, and I wrote every day. I wanted to achieve my dream of becoming a writer. I'm still working on that ambition to this day. Even when obstacles and disadvantages kept my grandpa from his goals, he found a way to overcome those barriers. I could do the same.

***

While writing this, I realized that it was time for me to stop moping and make the best of my circumstances. It was time for me to rise up. If I couldn't make a difference in the outside world with my presence, I would persevere with my words. I could make a difference with my stories. Maybe my writing could inspire people. Perhaps it could touch them in ways I can't even fathom. Or maybe just give them a spark of hope, like tiny embers bursting into flame. It's in dark times like these that we look for anything to tether us to hope, and sometimes that's half of the battle.

About the Author

Jamilette Pichardo was born in Puerto Rico and now lives in Florida. She has cerebral palsy and uses a wheelchair to move around independently. She graduated from Valencia College with an Associate's degree in General Studies. She then received her Bachelor's degree in English Literature from UCF. Before the coronavirus hit, she worked as a substitute teacher for OCPS. She's worked as a substitute teacher for eight years.

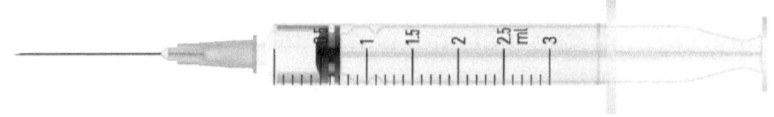

PANDEMIC

The hospitality sector was particularly hard hit by the COVID-19 pandemic. Many areas banned in-person dining, except for a brief period when outdoor-only dining was allowed. Restaurants had no choice but to pivot to takeout and delivery only. It was good for the delivery services, but bad for the restaurants, who saw their profits tumble. (asiandelight / Shutterstock.com)

PANDEMIC

"Since June 2020, 214 human cases of COVID-19 have been identified in Denmark with SARS-CoV-2 variants associated with farmed minks, including 12 cases with a unique variant, reported on 5 November. All 12 cases were identified in September 2020 in North Jutland, Denmark. The cases ranged in age from 7 to 79 years, and eight had a link to the mink farming industry and four cases were from the local community."

World Health Organization (WHO). November 6, 2020.

COVID-19

Scott Tilley

During 2020, I turned much of my attention to the novel coronavirus and COVID-19. I wrote several columns about the pandemic as part of my "Technology Today" series. This chapter contains an edited version of selected articles that reflect various aspects of our changed world, from fake news to new terminology to YouTube playlists.

Fake News

Do you remember the tag line, "Is it live, or is it Memorex?" It came from an advertisement in 1981 for the cassette tapes made by Memorex. (This begs the question: Do you remember what a cassette tape is?) The implication was that the recordings were so realistic that they were indistinguishable from the real thing.

Today, we find ourselves asking a similar question, except we're not talking about cassette tapes but news articles. How do you know something you've heard, read in print or online, or watched on TV is true?

Sometimes, satirical websites like *The Onion* run stories that are so close to being possible that it's difficult to tell. Other times, the story's source is obscured, leaving you to wonder, could it be true?

We've been barraged by information and commentary regarding the novel coronavirus (COVID-19) for almost a year. Fake news about the virus is spreading faster than the virus itself. It's been said that the best lies are half-truths, and stories about COVID-19 often follow this dictum. Here are seven stories about COVID-19 that made the rounds; I'll let you decide if they are truthful or not.

Drinking Corona beer can give you the coronavirus

This seems self-evident since the very name of the virus is part of the beer's branding. Who knows what goes into the water used to make the beer in Mexico? How come there's been so little reporting of people in Mexico testing positive for COVID-19? Do they have a natural immunity to the virus due to years of imbibing this famous brew? Is it part of a nefarious scheme to get back at the US for the revised NAFTA agreement?

Coronavirus was smuggled from Canada by Chinese spies

In 2019, the RCMP "escorted out of the building" several scientists of Chinese origin who were working in a biosafety level 4 laboratory in Winnipeg (the only

BSL-4 lab in Canada). These scientists had made numerous trips to and from Wuhan, China, the epicenter of the COVID-19 outbreak. The logical conclusion seems obvious: they perfected the virus in Canada while secretly working with Chinese intelligence to smuggle the secrets back to the mainland. If so, it would be one of the most significant examples of industrial espionage in modern times.

COVID-19 can be caught from swan poop

This might be true since we all know that swans are vicious beasts bent on world domination. If they have figured out a way of becoming a coronavirus carrier without becoming infected themselves, they will do it. Unsuspecting people at city parks would be targeted. Not only would the swans chase people across the fields, gnashing their sharp teeth in glee, but they would leave a trail of virus-laden pellets across the grass for unsuspecting people to step in, and that would be that. I've said it before: Don't trust swans!

Humans got the coronavirus from eating bats.

I'm not sure why eating bats would be on anyone's bucket list, but it seems it's a popular dish in parts of China around Hubei province (and elsewhere), which is where COVID-19 originated. Bats are unique creatures: they can carry a virus (such as rabies) without getting sick themselves. They are the flying equivalent of

Typhoid Mary.

If people ate infected bats in their soup, the virus could have jumped from animals to humans. There's a related theory that people ate snakes (Cobras), which had eaten the bats, and got infected that way. I'm not sure which scenario is more disgusting. Remember: SARS originated from people eating civet cats in Guangdong, China.

A coronavirus vaccine already exists.

This theory is based on the fact that Wuhan also has a BSL-4 laboratory. This would make COVID-19 a bioweapon, and no sane organization would make a bioweapon without also making a counter agent. (I hope.) Whether or not the virus was released accidentally or on purpose to disrupt the entire world is unclear (and dependent on your level of paranoia).

If the vaccine did exist, the Chinese government could not release it (yet) without giving away the truth behind the origins of the virus. This is similar to the situation the Allies faced in World War II when they had cracked the Nazi's Enigma codes but still had to let cities like Coventry be bombed for fear of giving away their strategic advantage.

The coronavirus is the result of 5G networks.

China has been rolling out 5G network infrastructure since 2019, including around Wuhan. Many people around the world think cellular towers and smartphones give off damaging radiation – and these people are not just members of the tinfoil hat brigade. The use of 5G, which significantly increases wireless network speed, presumably makes this radiation even more deadly. Wuhan residents have been subjected to 5G for much longer than we have, so they were the first to succumb to its ill effects.

I'm not sure why companies like AT&T and Verizon would want to poison us in this way since it seems rather detrimental to their business, but I guess it's a price we have to pay to watch our cat videos on YouTube without any delay.

Drinking cow urine will cure COVID-19

This advice comes from India, where cows are revered. I'm not sure who was the first person to experiment with this procedure, but good on you, mate, for advancing the state of science! In fact, they say consuming cow dung has an equally beneficial effect, and I'd agree with that. Just don't forget to chant "om namah shivay" while you do it; otherwise, you will not receive the full effect of the balm. Obviously.

***

Which stories from above about COVID-19 were true and which were fake news? The correct answers are:

- Drinking Corona beer can give you the coronavirus. FALSE

- The coronavirus was smuggled out of Canada by Chinese spies. FALSE (probably)

- COVID-19 can be caught from swan poop. FALSE (but swans are tricky beasts)

- Humans got the coronavirus from eating bats. TRUE (possibly)

- A coronavirus vaccine already exists. TRUE (now), but it wasn't clear at the start of the pandemic.

- Drinking cow urine will cure COVID-19. FALSE (but the advice from India was given in earnest, so who knows who gave it a try … ick!)

New Terminology

The novel coronavirus has already caused measurable changes in societal behavior worldwide. We avoid handshakes, hoard toilet paper, and watch the news in an almost obsessive manner. Hourly updates are full of dire warnings related to increased deaths, positive tests, and canceled events.

One of the more interesting changes has been the rapid introduction of new terminology related to the evolving pandemic. I'd hate to be a lexicographer these days; the rapid spread of the virus makes their job extremely challenging In fact, "pandemic" itself is a word fraught with peril, and I don't use it lightly. But unlike the World Health Organization (WHO), who seemed unwilling to use the word early in the virus' spread due to the likely panic that they thought would ensue, I think it's an accurate description of what is happening across the globe.

Here are a few of the new phrases that I've witnessed being commonly used in the context of COVID-19. I was not familiar with most of this terminology, but my profession is not medicine. The exception is "quarantine," which has been used in apocalyptic stories for decades (e.g., "The Andromeda Strain"). Now I regret not reading some of those "How To" books related to surviving zombie outbreaks.

Abundance of caution

I've already used this phrase myself. Early in the new year, I was teaching a course on "Writing Your

Memoirs" to a group of seniors at a local retirement/care facility. In February, I decided to cancel the class until further notice because I was doubly concerned: I didn't want to catch anything (I have a compromised immune system – see "underlying medical condition" below), and I didn't want to pass anything on.

I know of retirement homes that were forced to go into complete lockdown due to the spreading of infectious diseases like pneumonia and the anxiety it evokes in residents. I've also had to visit my sick father while I was wearing one of those dreadful surgical masks; it's not an experience I'm eager to repeat. The news of the deaths due to COVID-19 at the senior residence near Seattle in Washington State was the last straw; I canceled. Hopefully, we can restart later.

Social distancing

Humans are social animals. We crave contact with other people, both informal and intimate. Now we're being told to maintain a distance of at least six feet from other people in crowded spaces. I wonder how that's supposed to be done while traveling on a cramped airplane, a commuter bus, or a subway train. For people in Italy, many of whom are used to hugs and kisses as part of healthy behavior, this is proving to be difficult advice to follow – but the result has been skyrocketing numbers of sick people across the peninsula.

Social distancing has also led to the cancelation of numerous public events (e.g., SXSW in Austin – the first time in its 34-year history). I fully expected many other events would be canceled – and they were. Out of an "abundance of caution," we must plan accordingly.

Community spread

Many of the people who were infected with COVID-19 at the start of the pandemic acquired the virus through international travel. (The exception being Wuhan, China, where the coronavirus originated.) Just think about the sad souls on the cruise ships; it could easily have been you who was traveling on a bucket list trip that ended with invasive medical tests and lingering uncertainty (to say nothing of the extended quarantine periods).

There were also alarming cases where people have tested positive for COVID-19 without having traveled to hotspots like China, Iran, or Italy. Moreover, they didn't seem to have interacted with anyone who traveled. Such instances are called "community spread," and that's what health officials dread. When it occurs, we from containment to delay in dealing with the virus because containment is no longer be possible, and "social distancing" becomes even more important.

Presumptive positive

When the pandemic began, testing for COVID-19 was quite limited. Here in Florida, three labs (Jacksonville, Miami, Tampa) could perform the test. However, the test samples were still sent to the federal Centers for Disease Control and Prevention (CDC) in Atlanta for confirmation. During this period, a locally positive test is called "presumptive." As an engineer, I dislike systems with a single point of failure, and making the CDC a central chokepoint for testing nationwide was not sustainable.

Faster and cheaper testing procedures are under development, and a few have already been released. Still, the CDC technique relies on a "Reverse Transcriptase (RT)-PCR Diagnostic Panel" performed on specialized equipment as the gold standard. It requires a nasty delving into your nasal cavity to get a sample swab to work.

Underlying medical condition

Most people who are dying due to COVID-19 have an "underlying medical condition." The news media keeps using this suitably vague phrase to describe those at most risk, presumably to minimize panic, but what exactly does it mean? Basically, people with weakened immune systems (e.g., diabetes), respiratory illnesses, and chronic heart conditions seem to fall under this umbrella.

I'm in this category myself, and I don't take it lightly, but this is a pretty large group of people, and we're always more susceptible to illnesses. I'm not sure what I'm supposed to do differently for COVID-19 that I'm not already doing to avoid catching the common cold or the seasonal flu – with the notable exception of the lack of COVID-19 vaccine. For now. I hope.

Armchair epidemiologist

According to the US Bureau of Labor Statistics, "Epidemiologists are public health professionals who investigate patterns and causes of disease and injury in humans. They seek to reduce the risk and occurrence of negative health outcomes through research, community education and health policy." Choosing epidemiology as a career is rarely considered to be a good way of achieving notoriety. With COVID-19, epidemiologists have gained celebrity status. We listen intently when experts from the CDC give us the latest updates, and then we become armchair epidemiologists when discussing the news with family and friends. Sadly, this type of amateur speculation is the source of a lot of fake news.

Flatten the curve

Last year, I would have interpreted "flatten the

curve" to be some form of body shaming. Today, it refers to attempts to limit the peak of the coronavirus. The thinking is that a substantial spike in infections will overwhelm the healthcare system. If we can reduce that spike, the system has a better chance of coping. One way of flattening the curve is through social distancing, which is why so many parts of the country are going into lockdown. However, flattening the curve comes at a cost: the duration of the pandemic will be longer. It's a terrible choice to make.

Herd immunity

I first heard this term from the UK news. Several representatives from their National Health Service (NHS) talked about the need to achieve "herd immunity" to stop the spread of COVID-19. This is a phrase used in the context of infectious diseases that we're already familiar with, such as the measles. It's one reason experts recommend vaccinations: the majority of the population has to build up immunity to the infection to limit its spread. The NHS was talking about 60% for the coronavirus, but this approach seems to have been abandoned for now since it would require letting great swaths of the population become ill. Personally, I'm not sure I appreciate society being called a "herd" either, but then I witness toilet paper hoarding and shopping craziness, and I think perhaps the term is entirely appropriate.

Shelter in place

If social distancing is applied at a personal level, sheltering in place is an attempt to limit the spread of COVID-19 at the societal level. It is an extreme measure enacted by government agencies to force people to stay in their homes, with exceptions made for essential items such as groceries and prescriptions.

In the Spring, the Governor of California decreed that the entire state would be forced to shelter in place for at least two weeks. This means that nearly 40 million people saw their lives severely impacted, all in the hope of "flattening the curve." China did it, Italy tried, and France and the UK are doing it again (sort of). It's not a measure that we've ever experienced here before; time will tell if it's effective and if the gains outweigh the negative consequences.

Uncharted territory

Every time I hear a government representative announce a new measure that seems more attuned to wartime footing than regular life, they inevitably use the phrase "(We're in) uncharted territory." I find this phrase extremely alarming since it encompasses so many unknown developments. Fear of the unknown is a source of anxiety for most people. Sailing into uncharted territory is an apt metaphor for where we are now. Let's hope we find a new North Star to guide us through whatever lies just over the horizon.

Online Education

If you're like me, trying to follow the latest gloomy news about the coronavirus has become an anxiety management exercise. Of the many rapid changes to our lives, I find that the closing of colleges and universities and the subsequent moving of all classroom instruction to online platforms at extremely short notice is one of the more intriguing developments.

Online education goes by several names: virtual classrooms, distance learning, remote instruction, e-learning, and so on. Whatever it's called, online education is a marked departure for most faculty and students in traditional higher education. There have been online classes offered by most universities for several years, but they have usually been outliers, provided through an "extension" model that was administratively separate from the regular campus and departments. Now, we have major universities such as Stanford, UCLA, USC, Harvard, Princeton, Yale, and the entire Florida State public system moving their classes online en masse. As with most things related to COVID-19, we're in uncharted territory.

I've taught online classes in the past, and I can say from personal experience that it's very different than in-classroom instruction. There are indeed various tools available for instructors to tailor how their content is delivered, from live video broadcasts to recorded audio and PowerPoint presentations to chat rooms. But it's still quantitatively and qualitatively different from lecturing in a classroom, where the instructor can adjust presentation speed and style based on instant feedback from the students.

The whole topic of assignments and exams is another significant difference between online and in-person instruction. As a professor, I rarely used online assessments because I found the usual format of True/False questions somewhat limiting. However, some people become very adept at setting exams in this manner.

For classes with a hands-on component, such as a biology or chemistry lab, or a mechanical engineering course that does component fabrication, moving online presents unique challenges. There are virtual labs available for some computer science and engineering courses, where (for example) the workings of a network can be simulated via programs. But virtual labs have not matured across all disciplines to the same level.

Online education has long shared an interesting characteristic with artificial intelligence: its success is always "coming soon now." Has "now" arrived? Is this a black swan moment, arising unexpectedly and causing significant disruption? When the pandemic is finally over, will traditional bricks-and-mortar universities go back to their old ways of doing business, or will these changes remain for the foreseeable future?

If online education is seen as a success, I think students (and their tuition-paying parents) may demand more of it in the future. If there is no need for a physical campus, how much will fees drop? What would be the knock-on effect for institutions that rely on tuition to keep the lights on?

For faculty, how will their roles change? They are being forced to learn new tools and new pedagogical methods very quickly. How are students with special needs accommodated? Will online teaching speed up the adjunctification of universities' academic staff?

I've not said anything about the canceling of K-12 classes. Rolling out online education at this scale, in such a short period of time, can overwhelm parents and confuse students. (Indeed, it has.) For now, every family has to adapt to home schooling as best they can. Spring Break and other holidays can be fun, but when the break stretches into months, who knows what the impact will be on society.

Movie Theaters

The damage caused by the novel coronavirus (COVID-19) continues to escalate. There are, of course, terrible health risks, the economy is taking an unprecedented pummeling, and people's lives have been turned upside-down. As with all societal disruptions, there will be winners and losers, and the longer the pandemic lasts, the more pronounced I fear this schism will become.

Rather than focusing on one of the more severe consequences of COVID-19, I'll comment on one of the more innocuous pleasures we used to have: going to see a movie at the cinema. I've enjoyed going to see movies for as long as I can remember. I think the first one I saw as a child (in a church basement) was "20,000 Leagues Under the Sea" with Kirk Douglas. For a young boy, it was awesome.

I don't want to minimize the collateral impact of job loss from theater owners, ticket takers, ushers, and everyone else who is currently out of work due to the forced closure of all cinemas in the state; their losses are genuine and no doubt very concerning for their families. There is also a knock-on effect for everyone involved in movie production, from the writers to the actors to the distributors. But for now, I'll focus on the impacts on consumers.

In many ways, COVID-19 is just the last piece in a perfect storm puzzle that was already buffeting the movie industry. In recent years, most successful movies have been summer blockbusters, so-called "tent pole" releases. "Avengers: End Game" (2019) was probably the pinnacle of this type of movie, and although it was wildly successful (it's made nearly $3 billion worldwide), it was an outlier. A great many movies lose money, and recently, a lot of it.

**

This may be the curmudgeon in me talking, but one reason for the financial losses is the low quality of many movies released on the big screen. If you don't offer a product people want, they clearly won't pay for it. And with the cost of movie tickets going up, to say nothing of the astronomical costs of a small soda and bag of popcorn, a night out at the movies can become quite expensive. Throw in parking costs in many cities, the cost of a babysitter, and you're quickly into some serious money flying out of your pocket.

The second piece of the puzzle has to do with large widescreen TVs that almost everyone has at home. A giant 72" flat screen mounted on the wall a few feet away, coupled with a lovely (and inexpensive) sound system, rivals the experience at all but the largest movie theaters. Plus, the seats at home are usually more comfortable, you can pause for breaks when you want, and you don't need to keep shushing people around you to stop talking or texting during the film. Television and sound technology have made us more likely to choose a night at home over the hassle of a night out.

The third and final piece of the puzzle is highspeed Internet connections to the home and the streaming media services that have followed. Companies like Netflix have become ubiquitous around the world. For less than the price of two movie tickets, you can get a full month to binge-watch thousands of movies and TV shows, including a growing cadre of impressive original content. Why get off the comfy couch and leave your giant TV to line up for a so-so movie at the theater?

***

The "line up" (and seating) part of the experience is where COVID-19 comes in. Before the cinemas were forced to close, we had social distancing already in effect, with orders to limit attendance to 50% of theater capacity. By that time, I had already stopped attending group events. With the virus now spreading in the community, few people would want to take the chance of standing in line for tickets or refreshments, or sitting in close quarters with strangers, for two-plus hours. Hence the perfect storm: virus and health, large TVs at home, and a multitude of streaming services available at your fingertips.

The losers in this scenario are clearly the brick-and-mortar cinemas. Like theaters, bars, restaurants, theme parks, concerts, sporting events, museums, and others, they rely on people actually being there in person. For the time being, that's not going to happen. For a state like Florida, heavily reliant on entertainment and tourism for tax revenue, this will have a significant economic impact. Even luxury cinemas, which provide recliners, food and drink service, and added amenities, will have a tough time getting people back into the seats.

The winners are the consumers (us) and the streaming media companies. In addition to Netflix, Amazon Prime Video, Disney+, HBO Max, CBS All Access, and others have all seen a significant uptick in subscriptions. In fact, Netflix and YouTube report that Internet traffic has surged so much that they temporarily throttled bandwidth usage in Europe, which results in lower quality video. Conglomerates like Disney can benefit even more by offering their films in current release (normally at the cinema only) directly to the consumer for immediate rental or purchase. They are in the admirable position of owning the movie content, the movie company, and the online movie distribution mechanism.

The big question is, will people go back to the cinema when the coronavirus situation has settled down? On the one hand, there may be pent-up demand for social activities like going out to the movies, which could see people flock back to the theaters. On the other hand, people may have become accustomed to watching movies – including new releases – from the comfort of their own home. It would take a lot to overcome this inertia. And there's still the lingering feeling that the virus will be lurking somewhere, outside the safety of your nest.

Ironically, there is one form of movie theater that is already enjoying a renaissance: the drive-in. The great outdoors, a large screen, family and close friends in the car, and a night out that's not too expensive. My first memory of a drive-in movie is watching "Tora! Tora! Tora!" in 1971 while on summer vacation in Maine. With drive-in movies gaining favor, we may be going back to the 1950s – and perhaps that's not such a bad thing. Happy Days are here again!

April Fools

Is there anything that COVID-19 is not destroying? People's lives are in tatters. The economy is swirling the drain. And now, April Fools' Day has been unofficially canceled. The humanity!

In years past, I usually wrote about some of the amusing pranks from the technology companies when April 1 rolled around. In particular, Google put a lot of effort into creating masterful jokes that were Onion-esque in their tone: a bit out there, but almost real enough to be believed. Alas, 2020 will be known as the year that April Fools' Day forgot. Most companies are declining to provide an April Fools' joke for fear of being seen as insensitive. The few jokes that made the rounds this morning were rather lame or particularly tone-deaf.

There are so many FAKE NEWS articles already circulating about the novel coronavirus that making up new ones seems redundant. More importantly, such stories can be dangerous (and expensive). Did you read about the little hooligans that caused thousands of dollars of fresh produce to be spoiled by pretending to spread the virus through sneezing and coughing in the store? Haha indeed. True fools. Book 'em, Danno.

There are also warnings (from the FBI, no less – really!) about the dangers of using Zoom for videoconferencing. It seems there's a phenomenon called "Zoom bombing" where people attend your Zoom event uninvited, and they can do a variety of distasteful things. For example, sharing their screen with everyone else on the videoconference, and their screen inevitably displays some repugnant pornographic image that is guaranteed to shock and offend. Technology is always a two-edged sword, and there is never a lack of lowlifes trying to take advantage of the situation. Zoom is a great tool but use it with caution.

More than ever, in stressful times such as these, we need a bit of levity. So, I thought I'd share a story related to one of the FAKE NEWS items from a past missive. Do you remember the article that said drinking Corona beer can give you the coronavirus? This is obviously false. But is it possible that drinking Corona Light can give you just enough of the coronavirus to provide you with immunity? You know, the Goldilocks effect: not too much to make you sick, but not too little to have no effect. Do you think there is any truth to this rumor?

There's only one way to know, so I'm heading out to my pool deck to conduct a few liquid experiments. If this is a way to move us towards herd immunity, then I'm willing to do my part. The things I do for science. Besides, when the Governor issued a "stay at home" order for the entire state of Florida, else was I supposed to do?

A Pandemic Playlist

My horoscope (Pisces) for April 5 said the following: "To recognize when a thing is totally out of your control and act accordingly is good common sense and great leadership." I've never been accused of having an overabundance of common sense, but just in case, here come's some leadership!

In 2019, I wrote a column called "Like a Hurricane." It contained a hurricane-related music playlist for everyone to enjoy as we here in Florida nervously awaited Dorian's approach. The song of the same name from Neil Young was my favorite pick, but there were many other great choices. So many people sent me their selections that I've decided to create a similar playlist, but this time centered on COVID-19.

The novel coronavirus is no joke, but sometimes we have to rely on humor to get us through difficult situations. Seeing the absurdity in some of our actions helps give us perspective. There's a long-standing tradition of using mockery and satire to address things we can't control, and that's where we are now. Aided by technology, such as streaming media and smart devices in our homes, we're better prepared than ever to weather the storm.

So, in keeping with the spirit of spitting in the eye of the virus, here are seven of my choices (in no particular order) for songs that you can play on most music streaming services (and watch their accompanying videos on YouTube). From this list, you'll see that my tastes are quite eclectic. However, all the songs share a similar theme of endings – and of hope.

It's the End of the World as We Know It (And I Feel Fine) (R.E.M.)

https://youtu.be/Z0GFRcFm-aY

This is perhaps the ultimate "give the world the finger" song. It was released in November 1987. Michael Stipe, the lead singer, rushes through the lyrics, but when he gets to the main chorus, sing along!

That's great, it starts with an earthquake
Birds and snakes, and aeroplanes
:
It's the end of the world as we know it (I had some
time alone)

I feel fine (I feel fine)

V. Thirteen (Big Audio Dynamite)

https://youtu.be/sjqSRQoxnhs

Like "It's the End of the World as We Know It," V. Thirteen was released in 1987. I don't remember that year being particularly glum, but there must have been something going on to inspire two such different bands. To the endless irritation of my household, I've been playing this song every morning. Pay particular attention to the opening lyrics, which mention Sodom and Gomorrah, the "notoriously sinful cities in the biblical book of Genesis, destroyed by 'sulfur and fire' because of their wickedness (Genesis 19:24)." [Encyclopedia Britannica]:

Good morning Sodom and Gomorrah, good morning sinners

No, that wasn't your radio set on the bleep again
Sodom and Gomorrah, let the DJ play
'Cos I'm only gone tomorrow and here today...

Don't Fear the Reaper (Blue Oyster Cult)

https://youtu.be/q-XHvZKsLcY

Released in July 1976, this classic rock standard has been a staple of house parties and amateur bands for decades. SNL fans know that this version needs more cowbell, as Will Ferrell hilariously demonstrates: https://youtu.be/cVsQLlk-T0s.

All our times have come
Here but now they're gone
Seasons don't fear the reaper
Nor do the wind, the sun or the rain, we can be like

they are

Come on baby, don't fear the reaper
Baby take my hand, don't fear the reaper
We'll be able to fly, don't fear the reaper
Baby I'm your man

U Can't Touch This (MC Hammer)

https://youtu.be/otCpCnOl4Wo

Get your 90s back with this catchy rap song with great dancing and prescient lessons for social distancing. Can you still buy those pants?

I told you homeboy u can't touch this
Yeah that's how we're livin' and you know u can't touch this

Look in my eyes man u can't touch this

You know let me bust the funky lyrics u can't touch this

Until the End of the World (U2)

https://youtu.be/ejJdfkFjKCA

Staying in the 90s, U2's anthem from their 1991 album *Achtung Baby* was more personal. The lyrics tell a story of one person who misses the past and is oblivious to their current surroundings (much like people now who flaunt stay-at-home guidelines). The other person was already worried about what was coming. I'm not sure what approach is better.

Haven't seen you in quite a while

I was down the hold just passing time
Last time we met was a low-lit room
We were as close together as a bride and groom
We ate the food, we drank the wine
Everybody having a good time
Except you
You were talking about the end of the world

We Didn't Start the Fire (Billy Joel)

https://youtu.be/eFTLKWw542g

This song was released in 1989. Its lyrics are eerily accurate to our current pandemic. We didn't create or release the coronavirus, but we're stuck fighting it. And pandemics have indeed been around forever; this is just the latest incarnation. Let's hope it's also the last for a long time.

We didn't start the fire

It was always burning
Since the world's been turning
We didn't start the fire
No we didn't light it
But we tried to fight it

The Final Countdown (Europe)

https://youtu.be/9jK-NcRmVcw

A hairband from Sweden released this stadium-ready song in 1986. Turn on the flashlight app on your iPhone and wave it around as you sing along to this cheesy bit of fluff. Have fun with it!

We're leaving together,
But still it's farewell
And maybe we'll come back
To earth, who can tell?
I guess there is no one to blame
We're leaving ground (leaving ground)
Will things ever be the same again?

It's the final countdown
The final countdown

A Second Pandemic Playlist

Are we having fun yet? Here in Florida, by the time we reached Week 6 of our statewide lockdown, it felt more like six months of self-imposed quarantine. If it wasn't for streaming services that provide everything from movies to music to Zoom videoconferences, I think we'd all be going gaga. But this being Florida, how could you tell?

This is a second set of song recommendations to pass the time during the pandemic. You might as well enjoy them on YouTube now because I doubt any of us will be attending concerts in person anytime soon.

So, here are five more choices (in no particular order) for songs related to the coronavirus. For some songs, it's just the title that is thematic; for others, it's the meaning suggested by the lyrics. Enjoy this curated list of musical escapes.

Living In A Ghost Town (The Rolling Stones)

https://youtu.be/LNNPNweSbp8

These old guys are still rocking strong in 2020 with one of their best singles in many years. It was just released in April, but the Stones said they recorded it over a year ago while preparing material for their forthcoming album. If so, it sure was prescient!

Life was so beautiful
Then we all got locked down
Feel like a ghost
Living in a ghost town

I'm a ghost
Living in a ghost town

I'm going nowhere
Shut up all alone

Don't Stand So Close To Me (The Police)

https://youtu.be/KNIZofPB8ZM

The ultimate "social distancing" song, but with a somewhat ickier Lolita-related theme. Lead singer Sting used to be a teacher in England, so perhaps his experiences there influenced his writing on this hit from 1980. There's a remastered version of this song available online as well.

It's no use, he sees her
He starts to shake and cough
Just like the old man in
That book by Nabakov

Don't stand, don't stand so

Don't stand so close to me
Don't stand, don't stand so
Don't stand so close to me

Band On The Run (Paul McCartney & Wings)

https://youtu.be/t8dQwP80uNQ

An incredible song from 1973, written and performed in several parts. The first two stanzas directly address the feeling of being stuck inside. In this case, the writer was "sent inside," which in the UK means they are in prison. When I think of all the people living in cramped studio apartments (flats) today, I'm

incredibly grateful for where I live and the space I have.
But a pint would still be nice.

> *Stuck inside these four walls,*
> *Sent inside forever,*
> *Never seeing no one*
> *Nice again like you,*
> *Mama you, mama you.*
>
> *If I ever get out of here,*
> *Thought of giving it all away*
> *To a registered charity.*
> *All I need is a pint a day*
> *If I ever get outta here*
> *If we ever get outta of here*

Stayin' Alive (Bee Gees)

https://youtu.be/I_izvAbhExY

This disco-era gem from 1977 was one of the most memorable tracks from the *Saturday Night Fever* movie soundtrack. The music is excellent and suits the mood of John Travolta walking down the streets of New York. For our friends in New York City today, "stayin' alive" is a genuine concern. Thankfully, there are good Samaritans who have helped them.

Whether you're a brother or whether you're a mother
You're stayin' alive, stayin' alive
Feel the city breakin' and everybody shakin'
And we're stayin' alive, stayin' alive

Life goin' nowhere, somebody help me

Somebody help me, yeah
Life goin' nowhere, somebody help me, yeah
I'm stayin' alive

What Do You Want From Me (Monaco)

https://youtu.be/IhZKh0sXT1s

If there ever was a song written by a patient directly addressing COVID-19, it's this excellent tune from Monaco's 1997 debut album. It's a bass-heavy track, driven by Peter Hook's experience in *New Order*, that grows on you. The lyrics take on new meaning today if you imagine the writer lying in bed in an ICU ward, wondering how life changed so fast.

There is one thing. That I would die for.
It's when you say. My life is in your hands.
When you're near me. Your love is all I need.
Now I can't imagine.

What do you want from me?
It's not how it used to be.
You've taken my life away
Ruining everything.

A Third Pandemic Playlist

Here's a third "COVID-19 Pandemic Playlist" with a twist. All seven videos in this playlist are made using tools like Zoom and/or by amateurs who just want to demonstrate their talents by reinterpreting classic songs but in a coronavirus context.

More importantly, these videos were explicitly created to bring people together during the lockdown. The songs should make you feel happy. They should make you laugh. Above all, they should make you appreciate the immense talent and positivity that surrounds us all the time if we just look for it.

Lost Together (Blue Rodeo)

https://youtu.be/9yteNPh-boY

Original video: https://youtu.be/xAnJw9Ctqkc

This video was made available on CBC Music as a way of bringing Canadians together during this difficult time. There was a national vote, and this incredible song by *Blue Rodeo* was selected as representative of national ethos and what it's like being alone together in 2020. It's become the *Great Canadian Singalong*. The original video is from 1992. No comments on how the singers from Blue Rodeo have aged; we all have.

And I want all the world to know
That your love's all I need
All that I need

And if we're lost
Then we are lost together

Yeah, if we're lost
We are lost together

Do I Have The COVID Virus (The Barenaked Ladies)

https://youtu.be/tYk8dY2xrNo

Original video: https://youtu.be/UTK57dJc_pU

Sticking with the Canada theme, this parody of *The Barenaked Ladies'* hit "If I Had A Million Dollars" is very amusing. I like the fact that the little dog in the video seems to be enjoying the music as well. Is your temperature more than 38 degrees? (Celsius, of course.)

Do I have the COVID virus?
Should I self-isolate?
Do I have the COVID virus?
I've got to emulate
The health practices according to Health Canada.

Coronavirus Rhapsody (Raúl Irabién)

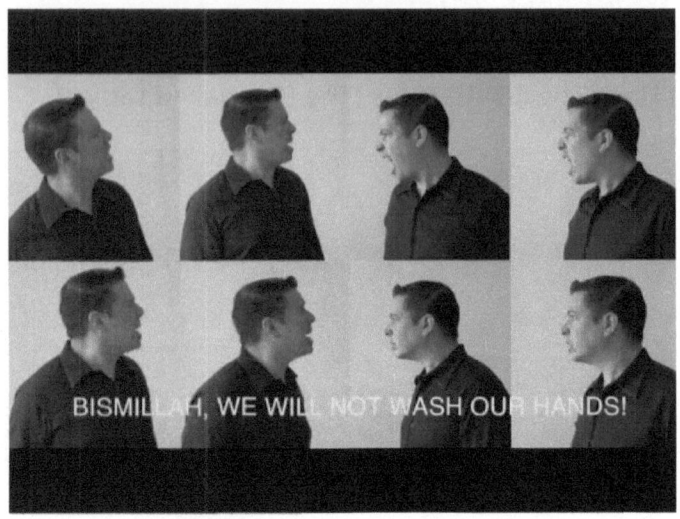

BISMILLAH, WE WILL NOT WASH OUR HANDS!

https://youtu.be/9Eo9M4-BrJA

Original video: https://youtu.be/fJ9rUzIMcZQ

Based on Queen's hit *Bohemian Rhapsody*, this fantastic video delights. There is only one singer, but his recording has been multitracked so that he actually harmonizes with himself. The lyrics are very witty as well.

Is this a sore throat?
Is this just allergies?
Caught in a lockdown. No escape from reality.
Don't touch your eyes.
Just hand sanitize quickly.

I'm just a poor boy. No job security.
Because of easy spread, even though
washed your hands, laying low.

I look out the window
the curve doesn't look any flatter to me.
To me.

Stayin' Inside (Brent McCollough)

https://youtu.be/nmUXntGlqFI

Original video: https://youtu.be/I_izvAbhExY

A coronavirus Bee Gees parody that is done Zoom-like with the musicians all playing in separate squares. The lyrics are great, and the singing is terrific. I bet your toes will be tapping along to this one.

Well you can tell by the way I wash my hands
I'm corona-free, won't take no chance

Toilet paper and latex gloves
I've been ready for this since I was born

And now it's alright, it's OK
You may look the other way
You can try to understand
The corona virus' effect on man

Whether you're a brother or whether you're a mother
you're stayin' inside, stayin' inside
Feel the city breaking and everybody shaking
we're stayin' inside, stayin' inside.

My Corona (Chris Mann)

https://youtu.be/ojrtwXqqc6g

Original video: https://youtu.be/kVdnqEyToqg

If you remember this 1977 hit from "The Knack," you'll appreciate this parody. I seem to recall wearing one of those skinny leather ties to parties and dancing away to this tune. I sure prefer the ties to the face masks.

I need toilet paper, toilet paper, toilet paper
My corona
I'm out of toilet paper, toilet paper, toilet paper
It's my corona

Got to make a grocery run
That sounds fun
I'm out here risking my life corona
Where's the parking space?

Shit, I touched my face
Wait, I think I finally caught my corona

Goodbye Corona!!! (Prairie Joe)

https://youtu.be/-2cFN2iC9u8

Original video: https://youtu.be/kVdnqEyToqg

What's better than one parody? Two parodies! This is a different take on the same song from *The Knack*. I love how the bass player is wearing rubber gloves, and all the kids in the band are wearing face masks. I can also relate to the cruises being canceled. Bummer!

Oh, I'm getting sick of this
I'm sick of this.
Why you trying to ruin my
life corona?

Oh, I want to take a trip

On a ship
but they went and canceled my
cruise corona.

Torn (Unknown, via the South China Morning Post)

https://youtu.be/6IOS7-4n12c

Original video: https://youtu.be/VV1XWJN3nJo

A parody of Natalie Imbruglia's song *Torn*. The setting and actions are all so accurate. Who has tried to open a door with your elbows to avoid touching anything? This video shows the pandemic is genuinely global.

So I'm kinda scared of being here.
There's lots of talking, lots of chatting,

without protective gear.
So all your germs are in the air.

During SARS I was just a child,
didn't seem to know, seem to care,
about the virus running wild.
But now I'm freaking out alright!

***

Quarantine (is Not Quite Over)

There is one more video that I feel must be added to the pandemic playlists. This is perhaps my favorite video of the COVID-19 era; I've used it in numerous talks to break the ice with meeting participants.

The video is "Quarantine (is Not Quite Over) - Billie Jean Parody" by The Holderness Family. It's a phenomenal music video that really captures what it's been like living in lockdown. I'm definitely the guy checking the mail. And maybe the hygiene-challenged person as well. Not good.

https://bit.ly/3nXxSgl

Each day is more like a creepy dream
from a movie scene
All day at home with my family
Can't see anyone

Put on pants ... get the mail ... turn around
Maybe go on a run...
See a friend, dive away, on the ground

Lifelong Learning

I miss doing live Tech Talks. I miss the background research and preparation, I miss the excitement of marketing and publicizing the event, but most of all, I miss the interaction with actual people. I've considered doing the talks online using Zoom, and I may still do so, but the lack of personal contact and audience feedback seems too limiting. With the coronavirus still circulating, I fear it will be quite some time before in-person presentations make their comeback.

So, instead of presenting material during the seemingly endless COVID-19 pandemic, I've spent a lot of my time exploring new areas of interest. With so much free time on my hands, it seems a waste only to watch Netflix and Amazon Prime all the time. There are numerous resources of fascinating knowledge available to anyone now, and I've availed myself of them over the last few months.

There are many online learning systems that you can try, such as Udemy, Coursera, LinkedIn – and, of course, YouTube. These are great sources for picking up new skills and possibly preparing yourself for a new career in the gig economy. Each course's costs are generally relatively low, or even free, but the quality does vary.

I prefer to consume this content in video format. I subscribe to services such as *CuriosityStream* as an add-on to my Amazon Prime account for a few dollars a month. They provide fascinating documentaries, mostly about science and history; they are quite watchable. I particularly like the physics and futurist talks by Michio

Kaku from the City University of New York.

But of all the sources currently available, I prefer the Great Courses material since it most closely aligns with the Tech Talks that I enjoy delivering. If you like the talks given by Florida Tech's "Lifelong Scholar Society," then I think you'll like these too. They are a series of college-level audio and video courses distributed by The Teaching Company. The courses cover a wide range of topics, from art to science to technology and more. The courses are delivered by professors who have recorded their lectures at The Teaching Company's production facilities in Virginia. It is like being in a lecture hall, listening to an expert discuss a topic in great detail. The lectures run for 30 minutes, but each course usually has about 24 lectures (there are a few that are shorter), so you're typically going to receive about 12 hours of excellent content. Pace yourself.

Until recently, you had to purchase each course, which you could then watch online or download to your computer. I did this for several topics I liked, and I found the quality very good. But the costs can quickly add up if you start buying a lot of courses. Thankfully, there is now a Netflix-like subscription model, called *The Great Courses Plus*, that you can purchase for $10 per month. This is an all-you-can-eat lifelong learning buffet, and it's terrific. (And, no, they are not paying me for this article.) The courses can be accessed online, but I prefer to use an app they provide for Apple TV so that I can watch from the comfort of my couch.

I spent a lot of time watching "The Black Death: The World's Most Devastating Plague," presented by Dorsey Armstrong of Purdue University. Over 24 lectures, she describes in great detail how the Great Mortality began its march across Europe, beginning in late 1347 and early 1348. The parallels to today's pandemic are eerie. Florence, Italy was hit by the plague 14 times over several hundred years; let's hope we're not in for such a terrible time.

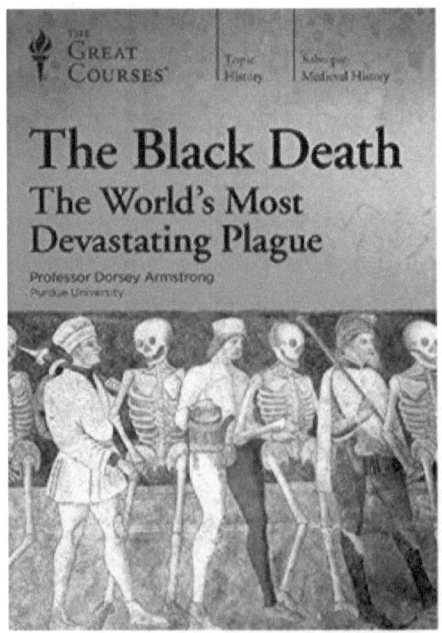

Some of the other courses I've watched over the last few months include:

- "Fighting Misinformation: Digital Media Literacy," presented by multiple professors

- "Understanding the Old Testament," presented by Robert Miller II of The Catholic University of America

- "World War II: Battlefield Europe," presented by David Stone of the US Naval War College

- "1066: The Year That Changed Everything," presented by Jennifer Paxton of The Catholic University of America

- "Einstein's Relativity and the Quantum Revolution: Modern Physics for Non-Scientists (2nd Edition)," presented by Richard Wolfson of Middlebury College

- "Understanding the Dark Side of Human Nature," presented by Daniel Breyer of Illinois State University

- "Comparative Religion," presented by Charles Kimball of the University of Oklahoma

As you can see, this is quite a diverse set of topics,

but that's one of the advantages of the subscription model. It makes lifelong learning a pleasure, particularly in these crazy times in which we're living.

About the Author

Scott Tilley is the president and founder of Precious Publishing, an emeritus professor at the Florida Institute of Technology, president and founder of the Center for Technology & Society, president and co-founder of Big Data Florida, Senior Fellow at the American Security Council Foundation, past president of INCOSE Space Coast, and a Space Coast Writers' Guild Fellow. His recent books include *Systems Analysis & Design* (Cengage, 2020), *Perspectives on Systems Engineering from Florida's Space Coast* (CTS Press, 2020), and *SPACE* (Anthology Alliance, 2019). He wrote the "Technology Today" column for FLORIDA TODAY from 2010 to 2018. He holds a Ph.D. in computer science from the University of Victoria (1995). Visit his website at http://www.amazon.com/author/stilley.

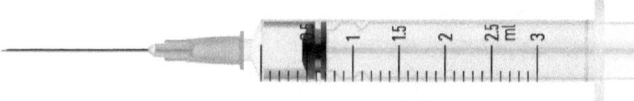

PANDEMIC

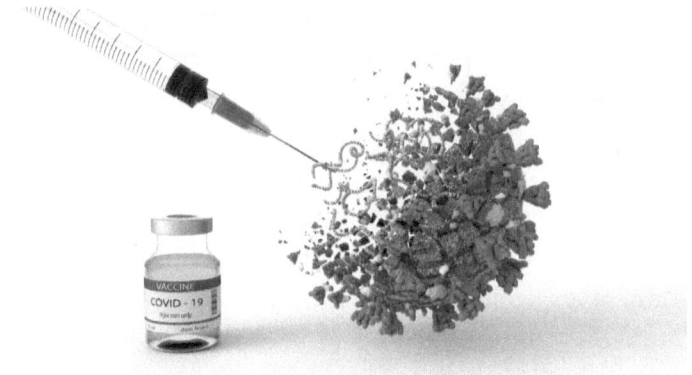

The light at the end of the COVID-19 tunnel is a vaccine. Fortunately, there are several in the pipeline showing promising results. It will still take many months to inoculate enough of the population to achieve herd immunity, and the antivaxers will doubtless confound the situation. The speed with which vaccines were developed is breathtaking: from inception to delivery in less than a year, as opposed to the usual 10-year cycle needed. (Orpheus FX / Shutterstock.com)

PANDEMIC

"Pfizer and BioNTech announced Wednesday that the efficacy portion of their Covid-19 vaccine trial has been completed, showing the vaccine to prevent 95% of cases of the disease.

The companies said that they plan to submit to the Food and Drug Administration for an emergency use authorization 'within days,' and will also submit to regulatory agencies around the globe."

D. Garde and M. Herper, STAT. November 18, 2020.

ANTHOLOGY ALLIANCE

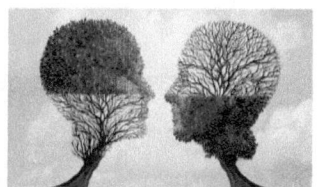

Anthology Alliance

The Anthology Alliance publishes collected volumes of work edited towards a unifying theme. If you are a writing group, a non-profit organization, or a school looking to assemble and publish a collection of your members' writing, contact us! We also work with aspiring authors to edit and publish short story collections, memoirs, and essays.

Anthology Alliance is an imprint of Precious Publishing. Precious Publishing specializes in taking your writing ideas from conception to fruition. We know that your stories are precious to you, and we'll do everything we can to help see your work published.

All of our books are available online from Amazon.com, usually in both print and Kindle formats. You are the author, we are the editor and publisher, and the world's biggest bookstore is the global distributor.

http://www.PreciousPublishing.biz/AnthologyAlliance

(diy13 / Shutterstock.com)